Jeremy stood transfixed when his match flared

He had gone to the Cherry Tart room, which he believed to be currently unoccupied, to relax and read while his friends enjoyed the Tart Shoppe's pleasures. He himself had not been in the mood.

And now he saw the sleeping form of a young woman on the bed, her robe parted to reveal a glimpse of splendid bosom and shapely thigh. Jeremy moved closer, then reached out to touch her veil of flaxen hair and run his fingers lightly over her cheek.

She moaned softly, and Jeremy tensed. Lord, but she was lovely! He knew she would be worth a fortune, but to his eyes she was an angel straight from heaven.

By all that was holy, he was going to have her....

Dear Reader:

Welcome! We're glad you joined us for our new line, Harlequin Regency Romance. Two titles a month, every month, for your reading pleasure.

We know Regency readers want to be entertained, charmed and transported to that special time of magic and mischief. And we know you also like variety, so we've included everything from the Regency romp to the dramatic and touching love stories that Harlequin is famous for. We offer you authors you know and love, as well as new authors to discover and delight in. We feel we have captured the Regency spirit and are proud and pleased to share it with you.

Harlequin Regency Romance was created with you, the reader, in mind, and we'd like nothing better than to know what you think. If there's something special you would like to see included, drop us a line. If there's any way we can improve, we'd like you to tell us. We welcome your feedback and promise to consider it carefully. After all, you are our biggest fan.

We hope you enjoy reading Harlequin Regency Romance as much as we enjoyed putting it all together. And, in the true tradition of the Regency period, "we wish you happy" and look forward to hearing from you.

Marmie Charndoff
Editor

THE TART SHOPPE
PHYLLIS TAYLOR PIANKA

Harlequin Books

TORONTO • NEW YORK • LONDON
AMSTERDAM • PARIS • SYDNEY • HAMBURG
STOCKHOLM • ATHENS • TOKYO • MILAN

As always, to Ed with love.
And with gratitude to the Thursday Group
Marion Wentzien, Marge Everitt, Pam Gullard,
Carol Culver, Jean Rossetta

Published June 1989

ISBN 0-373-31103-6

CHAPTER ONE

LADY CONSTANCE SEAFORTH huddled more closely into the corner of the carriage, feeling every bump of the cobblestones in the pit of her stomach. She couldn't go on like this. The pain worsened with each turn of the wheels.

She lifted her chin out of the deep folds of her travelling cloak and queried her chaperon. "How long will it be, Aunt Millicent? I can't abide much more of this."

Millicent Seaforth pushed aside the curtain and peered out into the night. "I can't truly say, child, but I fear it will be yet another hour. We've only now approached the far edge of London and the horses are tired from the long journey, I doubt they could be urged to greater speed."

Constance sank deeper into her cloak, holding her gloved hands across the base of her abdomen to help ease the pain. "I shall never, ever, as long as I live, partake of pigeon pie again."

"Try to sleep, Constance. Then perhaps you will be able to forget the pain." She tucked her hands into her fur-trimmed muff and leaned back against the burgundy upholstery. "Think of your lovely house and the furnishings you will buy to decorate it."

Constance closed her eyes, trying to shut out the grinding pain that threatened to overcome her. Her plans were finally coming to pass. For months she had been readying herself for the move from Cornwall to London. It had been two years since her father had suddenly taken ill and died three days later of progressive consumption. Her stepmother, Margretta, had worn the crepe for just over a year, then, on a whim, married a landowner from the colonies. She'd sold the family house in Cornwall in the firm conviction that her stepdaughter would follow them to the New World, but Constance had declined.

Now Constance was on her own. She often thanked a kindly providence for sending Aunt Millicent. Although Millicent had chosen not to marry, she had a nicely turned ankle and could have, except for a quirk of fate, easily acquired a suitable match without batting an eye. Truth be told, Millicent had never got over her infatuation for a secret lover. Rumour had it that he was one of the Royals, but she never confirmed nor denied it, not even to her closest confidants.

The waves of heat in the pit of Constance's stomach turned to ice, and a chill rippled down her spine. The home in London, she thought, her own beautiful stone house on Mount Street. If only she were there now, ready to crawl between the eiderdown quilts in the big four-poster bed.

For a stepmother, Margretta had been most generous. She saw to it that Constance had everything she could possibly want for years to come, assuming that Constance managed wisely or married within a reasonable period of time. Not much chance of that, though, Margretta had conceded. Constance was far too picky when it came to eligible men. Margretta had done her best to arrange a suitable match but Constance would have none of it.

She shifted her position and gasped aloud.

Millicent was immediately awake. "What is it, Constance? Is the pain stronger?"

"I...I'm sorry, Aunt Millicent. I...I cannot go farther. I simply must find a place to stay for the night."

"What will it be, then? There's no sign of an inn or a posting house."

"I just saw a carriage turn into that lane ahead," Constance said, peering out the still-open curtain. "It's a large place, lamps in several windows. There. What does the signpost say?"

Millicent lifted her lorgnette to her nose and read aloud the tastefully printed sign. "The Tart Shoppe, Tea and Cakes For Discriminating Tastes. They seem to do quite a business. Perhaps they also have rooms to let."

"Then please, do let's enquire. I simply must lie down."

Millicent turned around and opened the curtained window that separated the coach interior from the driver's seat. "Griswold, turn right into the next lane. We need lodgings for the night. Lady Constance is not well."

Millicent all but stuck her nose out of the window in the door as she studied the tidy flower beds, freshly painted bricks and grey shutters. "Yes indeed. This should do fine. That is, if they have room for us. They do appear to be quite busy."

A uniformed lackey stood at the entrance ready to lead the horses into the stable. He snapped to attention as a doorman dropped the steps to the carriage, opened the door and bowed.

Millicent reached for the handle to pull herself up and at the same moment the doorman met her gaze. "Oh, I say! Beggin' your pardon, mum, but I think you've made a mistake."

"No mistake, my good man. Take us to the concierge."

"But—"

"Do hop to it. My charge is ill and we have no time to waste." Her tone left no room for argument.

The doorman handed her down, then turned to help Lady Constance step onto the embroidered carpet that ushered them to the main entrance of the building.

"I must say," Millicent stated, "they do things up well. I'll wager this will cost us a pretty penny."

"Whatever it is, Aunt Millicent, let's pay it. I'm in no condition to bargain."

The doorman opened a black lacquered door into an elegantly appointed hallway, where they were met by a uniformed maid. She regarded them with something akin to amazement, but Constance put it to the fact that they were unescorted. Millicent took command.

"We shall be needing two rooms for the night, young woman, and quarters for our driver."

Freckles danced across the maid's face as she frowned. "I beg pardon, mum. Did you say for the night?"

"Yes, yes. Be quick about it, girl. My niece is not well."

The maid's gaze darted over to Constance, who was leaning against a lacquered table that held a large Egyptian vase. When it appeared the maid was still considering her next move, Millicent brandished her umbrella. "See to it, girl."

The maid bobbed a curtsey. "Yes, mum. I best call my mistress."

Through partly closed double doors Constance could see the tea room. White woven-willow chairs were positioned around a series of blue-linen-covered tables. Flowers graced each table; primroses and violets combined with bits of soft green fern. A few of the tables were occupied by beautifully gowned women and equally well-dressed gentlemen. The scent of freshly baked tarts filled the air with a delightful fragrance. Any other time Constance would have been sorely tempted, but now the mere thought of food sent her body into revolt.

She groaned and doubled over. At that precise moment an exquisitely gowned woman in silver-grey taffeta swept into the hallway, taking the two travellers into account in one bold glance.

Her cultured voice left no doubt as to her favourable upbringing, but her tone was less than sympathetic. "What have we here? Lettice tells me that you have insisted on renting rooms for the night."

Millicent regarded her with a fixed gaze. "That is so. And please do be quick about it."

"I regret to say that we have nothing available. The tea room is still open if you wish to partake of some of our heavenly apricot tarts before you depart."

Millicent drew herself up to an imposing five foot two. "Indeed. Are you saying that your rooms are completely filled?"

The woman smiled and made a moue with her mouth. "Not precisely. Suffice it to say that we have guests who travel this way on a regular basis. We cannot give the rooms over to perfect strangers just for one night."

"And I cannot subject my charge to another moment without rest. Lady Constance is quite ill. Would you prefer to see proof of that fact right in the middle of your lovely tea room?"

The woman looked quickly from Millicent to Constance, then to the extravagant Turkish rug that was centred on the floor. "Very well. Come with me. I have two small rooms left, but they are at opposite ends of the corridor."

"Well, that will never do!" Millicent stated flatly.

Constance clutched her aunt's arm. "Please. Let's not belabour the point. All I want is to fall into bed."

The proprietress lifted a bejewelled hand and motioned to several servants who had gathered to witness the exchange. "The Cherry Tart Room for Her Ladyship and the Banbury Tart Room for her chaperon. Ask Dormandy to see to the driver." She turned to Millicent. "Lettice will show you upstairs. I suggest you order dinner sent to your rooms if you wish to dine.''

She lowered her quizzing glass and patted her generous bosom. ''You have no abigail.'' It was a statement rather than a question. ''I trust that you will be able to manage. My girls will be otherwise occupied.''

Constance forced a smile. ''We can manage quite well, thank you. I truly appreciate your hospitality.''

The woman had the grace to look surprised. ''Indeed. That is kind of you, but I do hope you will make every effort to continue your journey as soon as possible.'' She inclined her head, then turned and walked away.

It was clearly a dismissal.

Millicent sniffed. ''The nerve of her. I've a good mind to give her a set-down she won't forget.''

''Do let's not concern ourselves, Aunt Millicent. In truth, I feel worse by the moment.''

Millicent motioned to the maid to take Constance's arm and together they helped her up the winding staircase to the next floor. The maid opened the door to the Cherry Tart Room and held it while the two women entered. She bobbed a curtsey.

''This is the larger of the two rooms, mum. The Banbury Tart Room is four doors down the 'all to the left. I'll show you meself.''

Millicent scoured the room in a single glance that missed nothing from the thick red Turkish carpet to the highly polished Empire mirrors and the pale pink coverlet the maid drew to the foot of the four-poster.

"Well, then. It will have to do, I suppose," Millicent said. She took the cloak from Constance's shoulders and hung it in the armoire.

Constance sank down on the edge of the bed. "It's quite comfortable, actually. I hope you will fare as well."

"Don't concern yourself with me, child. Sleep is what you need now."

"I shall try, but I doubt that I can fall asleep. The pain is too great."

"Then you must have one of my little powders." Millicent saw that Constance was about to protest and she raised her hands. "Yes, yes, I know. You don't hold with draughts and potions and pills. Never mind then, but I would sleep better knowing you were at ease."

Constance noticed for the first time the fine network of worry lines around her companion's eyes and she felt instantly contrite.

"I'll be fine, Aunt Millicent. Go on to your own room. I shall be sure to call if I need you."

"On one condition. That you drink a cup of herbal tea before you retire. It will settle your stomach. No arguments now. Do I have your word on it, child?"

Constance smiled. "I suppose it is the only way to get rid of you. Very well. I promise."

"Then I'll say good-night, but I'll expect you to send for me if you need me." Millicent grabbed the maid by the arm and led her to the door. Once it was safely shut, she rummaged in her reticule.

"Her Ladyship needs a powder to sleep, but she is stubborn beyond belief. Take her a cup of tea, but before you do, stir this packet of powder into it. Do you understand?''

The maid blinked twice and ran her tongue around the sides of her open mouth.

Millicent sighed, then extracted a coin from her purse and pressed it into the girl's hand. "Now do you understand?''

"Oh, yes indade.''

"And not a word to Her Ladyship.''

"On me mother's grave, mum.''

"Then see to it. If my charge sleeps through the night there will be another coin for you before I leave.''

The scattering of freckles seemed to fade as the girl stared wide-eyed. "She'll sleep through the night iffen I have to rock her in me arms, mum.''

Millicent drew a satisfied sigh and followed the maid down the hall to her own room.

OUTSIDE THE TART SHOPPE a closed carriage raced up the curved driveway and slewed to a stop. The team of matched bays pranced nervously, but the driver held them in check while the lackey lowered the carriage steps.

Inside were four men, three of them well into their cups who laughed and shouted with high good humour. The one farthest from the door grabbed at his neighbour's greatcoat.

"S-save the red-haired one f-for me. I've been holdin' back all week for th-that one.''

"Egad, Melton. You're too far gone to know what to do with her. But don't take alarm. The black-haired one with the little ring in her nose is the one for me."

Melton half fell out of the carriage, gratefully accepting the assistance of the first two men to alight. The third man, shorter by a good ten inches than the other three, slipped the doorman a coin. "For you, my good man. See that we're shown right to the mistress, would you?"

"Immediately, Lord Cheswick."

Cheswick patted his arm and turned to his chums. "As for me, I could take on the entire house tonight. What about you, St. James?"

The doorman snapped to attention. "My lord. Good evening. I didn't see you there in the shadows. Will you come this way, please?"

"Good evening, Webster. How is your little boy getting along?"

"Quite well, indeed, my lord. 'E's up and about most all day now."

Cheswick cut him off. "Well, St. James. Who'll it be? The French pastry or the German strudel?"

Jeremy St. James, the Earl of Marshfield, doffed his beaver and handed it to one of the maids who had assembled to assist the callers. "I told you before, Cheswick. I'm not in the mood. Madame Duprey has promised me a game of chess in the upstairs sitting room."

The three companions broke out in guffaws. Cheswick's roundly cherubic face split into a toothy grin. "I'll wager there'll be games all right, but it won't be chess."

Madame Duprey silenced them with a look as she swept down the grand stairway leading from the second floor. "Gentlemen, gentlemen, do keep your voices down. We have a full house tonight and we wouldn't wish to disturb anyone. Now, how may I help you?"

It took a while to assign them to their separate rooms. Jeremy St. James stood off to one side as they each departed on the arm of a beautiful and playful demimondaine. His mood settled heavily on his shoulders. It occurred to him that he had made a stupid decision when he had allowed himself to be talked into coming here again tonight. He was tired of it all. Tired of the gambling, the parties, the wine, the women.

He turned as Madame Duprey approached, a seductive smile lighting her dark eyes. He forced himself to act in a civil manner, but he wanted nothing more than to drop it all and rush home to his library and a warm fire.

"Jeremy, my pet." Madame Duprey stroked his arm through the burgundy velvet waistcoat. "Is there no one to please you tonight?" Her eyes glittered up at him through darkened lashes. "Perhaps it is up to me to bring you pleasure, no?"

He covered her hand with his, more to ensure that her explorations did not extend farther than out of true affection. He had tumbled more than once with the famous Madame Duprey and he was well aware of her hidden talents—and the streak of vengeance that she skilfully concealed from the unwary.

He shook his head. "You do me honour, Arabella. But I think not tonight."

"Then perhaps the game of chess we talked about?"

"I think, if you've no objection, I'll simply avail myself of a book until my friends are ready to depart."

Her eyes took on a hooded expression until he lifted her hand to his lips, lightly pressed it and said, "You do me a great honour, however, and I trust that I may avail myself another time."

She smiled thinly. "All you have to do is ask, Jeremy. I hope you know that." With a delicate flip of her gown she turned and floated toward the tea room.

He slowly let out his breath. He had saved himself after all. It did not do to say no to Madame Duprey, not if your tastes ran to the more exotic varieties of pastry. She was a powerful woman who was not used to being turned down.

Jeremy drew his hand across his carefully trimmed moustache. His mouth tasted of stale claret and the roasted squab in which he had overindulged at the club. He was alone, he was sober, and above all, he was restless.

It took one quick look in the library to change his mind about finding a book. The room was occupied by several prominent members of the beau monde and a bevy of light-skirted beauties.

Bernadette, his favourite, was not among them, and he recalled suddenly that she had gone to Ireland to spend a week with her mother. That would leave her room empty. What better place to find an hour's peace and tranquility away from the revellers. He took the stairs two at a time.

A quick glance inside the darkened room assured him that the bed was indeed vacant. He breathed easier, then closed the door behind him and reached for the gipsy matches, which he knew were kept alongside the heavy brass candlestick.

The match flared brightly, and in that instant something caught his attention on the floor at the other side of the room. He held the match higher. As the light steadied, Jeremy stood transfixed.

It was the body of a young woman. When she had fallen her robe had pulled askew, revealing a glimpse of splendid bosom and a smooth and shapely thigh. He stared at the softly rounded curves long enough to know that there was still life in that exquisite body.

He moved closer, holding the match aloft. Her flaxen hair spread out around her like a veil of pale gold silk. His hands burned to touch it, to scoop it up and let it cascade through his fingers like a river of gold.

She moaned softly and Jeremy tensed. Her eyes flicked open, and although they failed to focus, Jeremy felt an unaccountable lift of his jaded spirits. He turned to light the candle but the match chose that untimely moment to burn down. Jeremy sucked his scorched fingers, then swore competently. It was a bad omen, but not one to set him down.

It took a few moments to find the matches and light the candle, because his hands had begun to shake. Hardly aware that he was holding his breath, he leaned over her, then bent down for a closer look. He slowly exhaled.

How did it happen that Arabella Duprey had failed to mention this lovely new addition to her stable of girls? Was she saving her for one of The Tart Shoppe's famous auction nights? He swore softly. The girl would be worth a fortune, but the money didn't matter to him. He felt an incredible burst of excitement in the pit of his stomach.

He touched her hair, ran his knuckles lightly over the skin of her cheek. This girl was an angel straight from heaven, and by all that was holy, he was going to have her.

CHAPTER TWO

WHEN CONSTANCE next opened her eyes the room swam slowly in and out of focus. She darted her tongue across her lips and stirred uncomfortably against the pillows on the chaise longue. "Wh-where am I? What happened?" she enquired of the figure standing over her. Was he a flesh-and-blood man or one of the more pleasant consequences of the tainted pigeon pie? She was afraid to blink for fear he might disappear.

Jeremy tucked the robe around her feet and straightened. "Need you ask what happened? Luckily you forgot to stir the tea. There was enough laudanum settled in the bottom of your cup to send you to the grim reaper."

"Laudanum?" She pinched her eyes shut and passed her hand across her face to see if she were dreaming. She must be. She had taken no laudanum. And no man would dare invade the privacy of her bedchamber. Not even someone as handsome . . . She drifted off again, loving the fantasy. He was all the man she had ever dreamed of, even in her wildest imaginings. He stood tall and straight, cutting a dashing figure in his skin tights and Hessian boots. His raven-black hair curled softly against his ears. His eyes were dark and oddly disturbing as he studied her face.

Jeremy had it in his head to give her a good tongue lashing. But she had fallen asleep again, a secret smile lifting the sweet, temptingly kissable curve of her mouth. How dare she try to take her own life! True, the life of a demirep would not be easy, but she was so lovely. Surely she could have found a protector if she but set her mind to it. A few weeks ago he would have been first in line to make the proposition, but all that was over now. He had reformed.

He grasped his hands behind his back and strode to the window. The woman needed attention. She should not be allowed to drift back to sleep. She might, in truth, have imbibed more of the drug than he assumed. Should he call Madame Duprey? No. Instinct told him that Arabella would be livid if she discovered what had happened. The cardinal rule of the establishment was that no one, absolutely no one, be allowed to bring trouble down on the house. Reputation meant everything to Madame Duprey. One word of an attempted suicide and the girl would be out on the street or hauled off to Newgate Prison on some trumped-up charge.

He strode back to the chaise longue and looked down at her. His fingers remembered the satiny texture of her cheek. The sweet scent of lavender clung to his clothing where he had held her against him as he carried her to the chaise. He breathed deeply, letting the fragrance invade his head until it became a part of him. He bent down beside her, lifting her hand in his.

Her breathing had slowed. Was she slipping away? Dear heaven, he had to do something. Tea. He glanced at the pot on the tray and swore softly. In one smooth motion he sprang to the door and called for the maid.

"Tea," he said. "Quickly. Bring me three or four pots of it, hot and strong."

The maid looked at him oddly, then bobbed a curtsey.

"Hurry!" he shouted, and as she sped away he heard her mutter something that sounded like, "'Ot 'n' strong, he says. Next the likes o' 'im will be wantin' a whip 'n' cuffs."

Jeremy didn't stop to chastise the maid. He hurried back to the chaise and tried to waken the girl, but she was inert.

He grabbed her by the shoulders and shook her. "Wake up, miss. You mustn't go back to sleep. You've got to get up and walk."

There was no response. He picked her up and stood her on her feet, but her knees collapsed and she slid to the floor despite his efforts to hold her. Her head lolled against his knee and at the same time her robe pulled aside to reveal an enticing length of bare skin.

His palms began to sweat. "Devil and damnation," he said aloud as he felt the red begin to creep up his neck and into his face. He hadn't blushed since he was a boy. Why was this innocent-looking chit having such an effect on him? It had to be more than her looks. This wasn't the first time he had held such a prize piece of womanhood. But there was something about her. Something in the way her thick, honey-colored lashes dusted against her cheeks and the way

her silken hair curled softly against her damp forehead.

He swore again, then with one determined effort he
pulled her robe closely about her, picked her up, threw
her over his shoulder and dropped her none too gently
back onto the chaise.

Her eyes flew open and she gasped. "Oh!" Constance tried unsuccessfully to take stock of her sur-
roundings. The sudden contact with the chaise longue
had felt real enough, but she was still dreaming. He
was still here. She smiled and closed her eyes. If this
kind of dream came from eating tainted pie, it was
worth the pain.

Then she felt someone grab her roughly by the
shoulders and begin to shake her. She moaned. "Stop
it, stop it, I tell you!"

"Then wake up. No, don't close your eyes or I will
have to shake you again."

Constance forced her eyes to stay open, yet he
seemed to be fading in and out. Her voice sounded
thin and reedy, even to her own ears. She wet her lips.
"Are you real, then? I thought I was dreaming."

At that moment the maid tapped on the door.
"'Ere's your pots o' tea, sir. All four o' thim."

"Just leave them outside the door."

"Indeed I will, sir. I've no wish to see what you do
wi' thim."

While Jeremy went to get the tea, Constance dozed
off again. It took him several minutes to waken her,
and when he at last succeeded, he managed to get a
good half-dozen cups of tea into her, despite the fact
that she protested loudly and long.

He made no effort to question her. "No, don't try to talk now. Later, when you aren't so confused, you'll have plenty to answer for."

She looked at him with glazed eyes. The tea was getting to her. She had drunk a couple of cups before she'd gone to sleep. Now this moustached dasher was forcing her to drink even more. Her gaze skimmed the room looking for the chamber pot. She seemed to remember one, but what had happened to it? Perhaps the maid had whisked it way.

"What is it?" he asked. "You're worried about your mistress, are you? Don't worry. I shan't tell her. Your secret is safe with me."

She swung her gaze around to meet his and for a brief instant she focused her eyes on his mouth.

"My secret?"

"You've no need to pretend with me, young woman. I saw the laudanum. I know you tried to take your own life."

"I tried to—"

"Yes. I know. It was a stupid thing to do. Thank God I chanced upon you in time."

Constance was speechless. She slowly shook her head from side to side, but he cupped her cheek in his hand.

"Don't worry, little one. Whatever the cause of your unhappiness, I'll take care of it." He leaned forward and brushed a kiss onto her forehead. "I won't let anything happen to you. You're going to be all right now."

She would *not* be all right, she thought, until he left her alone to answer the call of nature. But she couldn't tell him that! Slowly the tears gathered at the back of her eyes and slid downward. One by one they began to roll over her cheeks in great, salty drops.

"My God!" he exclaimed. "What have I said? Did I presume too much?" He pulled a footstool close and sank down next to her.

She shook her head, afraid to move lest the pressure of the tea become too great.

He reached for her fingertips and caressed them with his lips. "Is it sleep you want now?"

She nodded quickly. "Yes. Sleep. That's it."

"Very well. I'll carry you to the bed."

She drew a sharp breath. The slightest movement and she would die of shame. "No, please. I . . . I prefer to sleep here."

"Very well. Then I shall position myself on the bed so that I can watch over you until you awaken."

"No... I...it isn't necessary. You are too kind, but I prefer to be alone."

"Nonsense." He dragged his hand across his moustache. "You see, I am not sure I can trust you...after what you tried to do. I think perhaps you should drink another cup of tea."

"Tea. Tea? Surely you jest." Her voice rose an octave.

Constance was at her wits' end. How could any man who looked so intelligent and so well put together be such an ignorant clod? She steeled herself to face him. "My dear sir, I have had enough tea to float the entire British Navy. If you do not leave me alone at once I shall surely succeed in embarrassing us both."

Jeremy jumped to his feet as if he had been sitting on a hot griddle. "Oh, I do beg your pardon. I didn't mean to... If there is anything I can do..." His face was as red as the velvet draperies. He wasn't sure if he was more angry at her or at himself for being put in such an untenable position.

Constance felt the beads of perspiration begin to pop out on her face. "Do just go, please."

"Yes, yes, at once." He backed toward the wall, then, feeling for the doorknob, jerked the door open and slammed it quickly behind him.

Later, when Constance managed to crawl back into bed, she lay awake for a long time thinking about the man who had invaded her bedchamber. He had the manner and bearing of a gentleman. Though he had the good grace to be embarrassed by the collection of circumstances, there was still an indefinable air of authority in the way he behaved. Obviously he was highborn. But what was he doing here? Did he have a proprietary interest in The Tart Shoppe?

The thought of food sent a spasm of pain through her midsection, and she groaned. Would she be well enough to travel with the coming of dawn? She bent her knees, hugging them to her chest. And if she were still too ill, would fate afford her the chance to see him again?

Him. She didn't even know his name. One thing was certain. A smile dimpled her cheek as she drifted toward sleep. She would at the very least learn his identity before she continued on her way.

THE HOUSE HAD HARDLY begun to stir the next morning when Aunt Millicent wakened her, nigh into a snit. "What do you mean, a man came into your room last night?" she demanded. Then she settled back. "Never mind. You must have dreamed it. I asked the maid to give you a draught of laudanum. It does that sometimes, you know. Makes one dream outrageously."

"But it wasn't a dream. I drank a cup or two of the tea and then the room began to spin and I tried to get up. The next thing I knew I was on the floor and he was standing over me. He lifted me in his arms and carried me to the chaise."

Aunt Millicent fanned herself quickly with a square of embroidered lace. When she again spoke, her voice carried easily to the other side of the room, where the maid was filling the basin with fresh water. "Just what kind of place is this that a man would be allowed to enter the privacy of a woman's bedchamber?"

Lettice straightened and looked surprised. "But, mum, it is *that* kind o' place."

"I don't understand you. Speak up. What do you mean?"

The maid started to back toward the door. Eyes wide, face flushed, her whole body registered distress. "'Tis The Tart Shoppe, mum."

"Do not be so obtuse. After all, I can read."

"Yes, mum. What I mean to say is this really is a...a house. A *tart house*."

Millicent was fast losing her patience when Constance started laughing, then quickly sobered. Millicent was far from being amused.

"And what is so funny?"

"Dear heaven, Aunt Millicent. I think what the girl is trying to say is that this house specializes in male visitors. We've stumbled into a house of ill repute."

Millicent's face lost every ounce of color. Her quizzing glass, which she had affixed to her eye to study Constance's face, fell to the end of its chain. She lifted her small bosom as if struggling for breath and at the same time fumbled in her reticule for her vinaigrette.

"Well! Well, indeed. I shall see about this. Young woman. Send your mistress here at once."

The maid scurried away without further ado and a short time later returned with word that *madame* would arrive presently. As soon as she delivered the message the maid slipped out the door, leaving the two women alone in Constance's bed chamber.

Constance lay back on the pillow. "I feel much too weak to travel, but I fear we have no choice in the matter. We must leave today before word of this gets out."

"I'll have the woman transported for this."

"Truly, Aunt Millicent. We can't rightfully blame our circumstances on the, er, madam. We did, after all, insist that we be allowed to spend the night."

"But . . . but . . . Well, the least she could have done was to keep her gentleman callers confined to . . . to certain quarters."

"Oh, he was very much the gentleman. He did, in fact, save my life. The maid must have wanted to be certain I slept, so she apparently gave me two packets of laudanum instead of one."

Millicent looked again as if she would swoon. "Oh,

my dear! What a dreadful mistake.'' She held the vinaigrette to her nose. "And no doubt she'll want another coin. But yes, I suppose you are right.''

"I'm certain of it." Constance pleated the satin coverlet between her fingers, at the same time contriving to look innocently demure. "Considering the circumstances, wouldn't it be better to avoid a confrontation with the, er, madam? The less said about the matter the better off we are."

Aunt Millicent sighed. "Dear heaven. If only we could have known what trials would befall us. Whatever shall we do? The gossips will have a field day with us, you know, once they hear that we have been compromised."

"Let me talk to the madam alone. I think we can come to some agreement about the need for discretion."

"Perhaps you are right. You do have a charming way with people. But do be careful what you say. In the meantime, I'll see to the packing."

Constance was rapidly tiring by the time Millicent finally left her alone. It was only moments later that Madame Duprey tapped at the door and entered. She had discarded the grey taffeta, wearing now a lavender morning gown of exquisite cut that was an excellent copy of one Constance had seen in a recent issue of *La Belle Assemblée*. The woman was no pauper.

She swept into the room, her arms folded in front of her. "My maid said that you wished to see me. I presume you will be ready to travel before the noon hour?"

"We plan to leave as soon as we are dressed and packed."

"A wise decision."

Constance smiled in spite of herself. "Yes. I agree. We didn't realize last night what kind of place this was. I trust we didn't inconvenience you too much. I also trust that you will be so kind as to protect our family name from unnecessary publicity."

Madame Duprey pulled her shawl around her shoulders. "We are always discreet, Lady Constance. I see no reason to make an exception in your case. I'm sure no one saw you, save for two or three of my servants. They will not talk."

"There was a gentleman who paid me a visit last night."

Madame Duprey dropped into a chair. "Indeed! Surely you jest."

"He was very tall and darkly handsome, with a close-clipped moustache. A fine figure of a man. Wearing wine-coloured breeches that fit snuggly...." Constance cupped her hands in an eloquent gesture that spoke more than words.

"Jeremy St. James was in your room?" Madame Duprey's jaw dropped as she considered the possibilities. Had the cad turned her down simply because he saw fairer game waiting down the hall? The nerve of him.

Constance saw that the woman was distressed. "I assure you, *madame,* he was the perfect gentleman."

"I find that hard to believe. Jeremy St. James has the reputation of a rakehell and a womanizer. To put it kindly."

Constance nearly gasped. "That was Lord Jeremy, the Earl of Marshfield?"

"You've heard of him, then?"

"Is there a woman under five-and-sixty who hasn't? No wonder he had the gall to come into my bedchamber without so much as a by-your-leave."

"I doubt that you had anything to worry about. He claims to be a reformed man."

Constance laughed sharply. "Indeed? Then he came here to play checkers, no doubt?"

The madam leaned back in the chair, a sly smile lighting her face. "Chess, actually. No. The truth is that he was waiting for his friends. We seem to be out of favour with him for the present, though I warrant I offered him the best of the house. Men! They take what they want but how soon they tire of their playthings." She made a delicate gesture with her hands and both women smiled.

It occurred to Constance that she could not readily dislike this woman. There was a certain honesty about her, coupled with a wry sense of humour that was strangely appealing.

Constance traced the satin coverlet with her fingertip. "My father was a womanizer until the day he died. My mother was beautiful, as was my stepmother, but they were never enough for him. He always needed a bit of fluff on the side." She rolled onto her back and studied the carved and sculpted ceiling. "I wouldn't stand for that. When I marry, my husband must be true to me. Perhaps that accounts for the fact that I've been slow to give the nod."

"It's reason enough, my dear, assuming you have the funds to live the way you wish without a protector. As for myself, I've no desire to be any man's property. If I give them what they want it is with the clear understanding that they pay the price." She smiled, fluttering her hands to display a marvelous collection of jewelled rings.

Constance fixed her gaze on the woman's downcast face. "And Lord Jeremy. Does he pay?"

Madame Duprey looked up sharply. "I don't believe it is any of your concern. But tell me, do I detect more than the usual curiosity?"

"No, I..." Constance realized she couldn't fool this woman. "Yes. I do confess to a rather significant measure of interest. Blame it on the laudanum."

"Be advised, then, that Jeremy is not the marrying kind. He would only bring you pain."

"No need to worry. I'm not likely ever to see him again. And if I did, it would only be to give him a proper set-down."

Madame Duprey nodded. "You are not only lovely, Lady Constance, you are intelligent. Forgive me if I speak too freely, but I have the distinct feeling that, given other circumstances, we might have become good friends."

"I would have liked that," Constance said. She truly meant it.

"Thank you. You are most kind." She rose. "I doubt that I'll be seeing you again. Be careful to close the curtains on the carriage before you leave the stable. You must understand the possible consequences, should word of your stay here become public knowledge.''

"I doubt that idle gossip can harm me."

"How wrong you are, my dear. To believe yourself above gossip is to be naive beyond belief. Polite Society is at best a ruthless taskmaster."

She stepped back inside and closed the door. "Again, I promise you this. No one will ever learn who you are from me or my servants. You have my word on it." With that she went out and closed the door softly behind her.

THE LAMPLIGHTER had scarcely extinguished the torches leading up the cobbled drive before Jeremy St. James arrived the next morning and went directly to Arabella Duprey's private quarters. She answered his knock and curtsied as he entered the room.

"Since when do we stand on ceremony, Arabella?" he asked, bending to brush her fingers with his lips.

"Since you have been so strangely out of sorts. What is it, Jeremy?" she asked, motioning him to a chair. "Just what have we done that so displeases you? Is it my girls? Have they been disrespectful? Uncooperative? Indeed, it has been so long since you have sampled our wares that I warrant you can't even recall the reason."

He adjusted his breeches and crossed his legs. The highly polished Hessians glinted darkly from the shaft of sunlight that filtered through the partially drawn curtains.

"I assure you, Arabella, that neither you nor your girls have anything to do with it. I cannot account for my severe attack of ennui. I simply lay it to the fact that I have tasted all that there is to offer and there is yet something missing. For weeks now I have stepped back to play the observer, hoping that some inner sense will guide me toward what I've missed."

"Indeed. It seems more like months instead of weeks. And have you discovered the source of what you so passively seek?"

His eyes darkened. "In truth, no." He laughed. "But it has saved me a king's ransom at the gaming tables."

Her voice was dry. "Am I to believe that you truly have reformed? That you take no more pleasure in gambling or in lifting the skirts of a pretty young chit?"

He moved uncomfortably. "There is partial truth in what you say, but I must confess now the true reason I am here so early."

"I knew there was something behind this sudden reformation."

He looked wounded. "Arabella, how cruel you are when you know you have me in an indefensible position."

Her heart skipped a beat. "Just what is it you want from me, Jeremy?"

He stroked his moustache, then leaned forward, resting his elbows on his knees. "I want to buy out the rights to the new girl you've hidden away upstairs. I'm willing to pay off her debts, all of them, and give you a generous commission, as well. But I must have her, Arabella. I must."

CHAPTER THREE

ARABELLA STIFFENED. Then she stood and walked toward the darkened window. It was some time before she turned to face Lord Jeremy, and when she did he was ill prepared for the expression of contempt in her eyes.

"You want me to sell her to you, is that it? So much for your reformation. I'm disappointed in you, Jeremy. Truly disappointed." Her penetrating gaze didn't leave his face as she tucked her hands into the folds of a lace-and-cashmere shawl. "And the answer is no. The young woman is not for sale." She smiled at his obvious disbelief. "Besides, if she were available, even you, Jeremy, with your extensive holdings, would be quite unable to afford her."

"Don't underestimate me, Arabella. Since you refuse to discuss it, I'll go directly to her."

"As you wish, but I vow, Jeremy, you'll rue the day."

He straightened. "I intend to take her out of this place if I have to drag her. I warn you. Don't try to stop me."

Her eyes glittered at the prospect of revenge. "Stop you? No, Jeremy. I wouldn't dream of it. Now suppose you leave before I lose my temper."

He turned and strode from the room, slamming the door behind him. His heart sounded as loud as a smithy's hammer in his ears. Could he trust Arabella to let him take the girl without any interference? In the past he had heard of more than one occasion when Arabella had called out her gang of toughs. Now she was angry enough that she might do anything. He had to get the girl out of there before Arabella had a chance to alert her ruffians.

The door of the Cherry Tart Room was closed. That was to be expected. Mornings found most of the house sleeping in. But as he neared the room he heard movement. He swore softly. If there was a man with her he would kill him.

The thought shook Jeremy, and he stopped in his tracks. He was by nature a quiet man, not prone to violence toward any living thing. What kind of woman was she that she could awaken such protective urges in him? He mopped his brow with the back of his hand and looked at the door. It was now or never. If he didn't save her this moment, there was no telling what manner of revenge Arabella might take against her.

He knocked shortly on the door and entered without waiting for an invitation.

Constance was just finishing the buttons on her blue travelling dress and she didn't bother to turn around, thinking it was Millicent who had entered the room. When there was no response to her greeting she turned abruptly.

"You! What are you doing here? Really, sir, you should do me the courtesy of waiting to be invited before you enter my room. Do go at once before someone discovers you here.''

"It's all right. Madame Duprey knows I am here."

"That does not signify. It certainly is not all right with me."

"I mean you no harm. There is no time to waste. I only came to help you."

"Help me? Unfortunately, my lord, your reputation puts the lie to that statement."

"Please do not be so quick to judge. I want to take you away from all this, but we must leave at once before Arabella calls out her thugs."

"You, sir, are the one who must leave before my chaperon sees you. She can be as protective as a wounded lioness."

He laughed out loud. "Truthfully now, you don't really have a chaperon, do you?"

Her eyes regarded him with confusion. "Most certainly I have a chaperon. Why should that come as a surprise?"

"You're right. Nothing Arabella does these days surprises me. On the other hand, you are not still so young that society must dictate the need of a chaperon." He regretted his words the moment he said them, but he didn't know how to handle this prickly young woman.

Constance tensed. "I beg your pardon, sir. Are you being so crude as to ask how old I am?"

"That wasn't my intention, but now that you mention it, just how old are you?"

"Old enough to know better than to be taken in by men such as you. Now be kind enough to leave before I call Madame Duprey and have you thrown out."

"You don't understand." He fumbled with his high starcher, which this morning seemed to be too tall and too stiff. At least, something was making it hard for him to breathe. "Look, why don't we sit down and discuss this? Truly, there is danger. We haven't much time before we must leave."

"We?" Constance dropped the small leather dressing case she was holding. "Did you say *we* have to be leaving?"

"Yes. That's what I've been trying to tell you. I had a long chat with Arabella this morning and she has finally agreed to release you. I'm taking you with me. I've decided to become your protector."

At that Constance sat down—abruptly. He saw the look of shock on her face and he smiled with the touch of smugness that comes only from a lifetime of having one's own way.

"Dash it all. I haven't even thought to ask your name."

"You've decided *what*?" she demanded.

He shuffled his feet in a decidedly boyish gesture. "How shall I explain? The truth is that when I found you on the floor last night I was completely taken by you and . . . and your plight. From the moment I saw you I wanted to take care of you, see that no one had a chance to lay his filthy hands on you again."

"Oh? Oh! Now I see. What you are telling me is that you want to reserve those rights for yourself. Is that not so? You wish to have complete control over me while you are—how did you say it—protecting me." Her whole body shook with anger. "Knowing who you are, sir, I suspect I would feel more protected in the confines of The Tart Shoppe."

She rose, grabbed her hairbrush and flung it at him. "Now get out of here." The brush hit him squarely on the chest. He ducked when he saw the hand mirror coming toward him. When she picked up the leather case he moved toward the door and opened it. Only quick action enabled him to close the door behind him before the solid leather case struck wood with a resounding thud right at head level.

Jeremy was confused and more than a little unsettled. Why had she reacted so violently? Most demireps and demimondaines would have given anything to spend a day, a week, a month, under the benevolence of his protection. Just what was it that made her so excitable? Could he risk waiting until she had calmed down? Perhaps that was best. He would approach her in an hour or so, when she had recovered from her near brush with death. Then perhaps she would me more amenable to his suggestion. Confound it, though. He still had not learned her name.

Two hours later, when he again came to The Tart Shoppe, laden with a bauble or two and a box of bonbons to sweeten the bargain, he found her room empty. Worse yet, no one seemed to know her name or where she had gone. Bribery availed him nothing. Either the maids and grooms were incredibly stupid, or Arabella had threatened them with certain death if they revealed any knowledge of the woman's whereabouts. Jeremy begged, even humbled himself before

Madame Duprey, but she was unrelenting. She had vowed that he'd rue the day. Now she seemed determined to make good on that threat.

AFTER THE EARL had left her room, Constance made haste to complete her departure before he decided to return. An occasional wave of nausea continued to plague her, and once or twice she had to rely on a vinaigrette to keep from fainting. The pigeon pie coupled with the overdose of laudanum had taken their toll, but her anger sustained her. In a little over an hour their carriage approached The Beeches, her home on Mount Street.

Constance awakened from a short nap and looked out the window. "We're almost there, Aunt Millicent. Home! Oh, how I love this place. It's been so long since I was here."

"Seven years at the very least. Your stepmother loved Cornwall and was content to live there, but we can thank her for keeping this house up instead of letting it go to ruin."

"I think of The Beeches as my mother's house, the place where I grew up. But I loved Cornwall, too, and Margretta."

"There. You can see the chimneys and the beech trees from here."

"Look how the trees have grown. The street seems narrower somehow."

"Everything looks smaller after you grow up."

The carriage turned a corner and the grounds came into view. A six-foot-high wall of weathered stone marked the perimeter of the property. Forsythia and bridal wreath vied with ivy, which spider-webbed its way among the loosely mortared stones. Beyond the wall, beech and maple trees stood in a parklike setting, dappling the spring-green turf in shadow. It was the trees that had given the house its name.

The carriage slowed and came to a stop in the gravel driveway. The carriage shook slightly when the lackey jumped to the ground and flung open the door, and put down the steps.

He grabbed his cap and held it between his hands. "Here we be, miss. And right good time, too. Aye, and it's a bonny house, too, just like you said."

Constance accepted the hand he offered and alighted. "So it is, Angus. A bonny house. I hope you like it here."

She stood for a moment, taking it all in: the grey stone house, its gables and shutters freshly painted a sparkling white. Centred above the wide, double-door entrance was the Seaforth family crest. The shield of black was divided unequally by a red trident, a grey sea serpent and a gold crown. The stories her father had told her about!

Her memories were interrupted by Mr. and Mrs. Stavers, who, upon seeing the carriage arrive, rushed out to meet them.

From then on until time for bed, the house was a blur of activity. The Stavers, butler and housekeeper to the Seaforth family for more than thirty years, had done their work well. A temporary staff, hired to clean the house after the tenants had moved out, were staying on until such time as Lady Constance should make a decision. She was content with things as they were.

Running a house had never been her penchant. She much preferred to work at her drawing. A sketch pad and assortment of fine leads were never far from her hand.

But as Constance settled into the eiderdown quilts that night she thought of little else than Jeremy St. James. No wonder women found him irresistible. One look from those indigo eyes and his spell was cast. She told herself to stop thinking about him. He was an arrogant, irresponsible cad who cared nothing about anyone but himself. And he wanted to become her *protector*. Indeed! Her only regret was that she had neglected to tell him her true identity. He would have been mortified.

She sighed. To be truthful, it wasn't her only regret. Her experience with men was somewhat limited, but she knew what men wanted from women. What it was that *women* wanted, she wasn't quite sure. Of course there was security. But she had security, assuming she was somewhat prudent. Still, there was an indefinable something that nagged at her whenever she thought about the handsome earl. A warming in the pit of her stomach. A breathlessness as if something were waiting to happen.

She pulled the covers up to her chin and counted the crystals in the chandelier that hung in the window alcove at the foot of her bed. Tomorrow and the weeks ahead would be filled to capacity. She couldn't waste her strength on idle dreams that would only disturb her peace of mind.

The next few days passed as quickly as lightning in a summer sky. There was still much to be done before

Constance and Millicent could entertain visitors. True, a number of cards had been received, but so far the women had not set an ''at-home'' day.

Mrs. Stavers, her white hair so thin that her scalp gave the hair a pinkish tinge, insisted daily that Lady Constance do something about the draperies in the drawing room. The sun had faded stripes into them where they should have been a solid, dusky rose. ''And they smell like a musty trunk,'' she said every time she walked past the room.

On Wednesday afternoon Constance set out with Millicent in the town carriage for a trip to Harding, Howell, and Company, the linen drapers on Pall Mall.

The store, with its bolts of fabric piled nearly as high as the ceiling, was crowded with shoppers when they first entered. A harried clerk, his face as pale as if it had never seen the light of day, apologized for not coming to their aid.

''Never mind,'' Constance said. ''We want to take time to select just the right fabric.''

He looked enormously grateful.

They found it after a while: a soft, shell-pink velvet that would blend in beautifully with the China rose of the upholstery and the deeper burgundy rose of the Oriental rugs. Constance pulled out her sketchbook and showed the clerk a sketch she had made of the window arrangement. He agreed to send a seamstress by within the week to begin work.

The shop had cleared somewhat by the time the clerk was looking up her father's account, but there were a few customers who browsed casually through the stacks of fabrics.

One woman's attention had been caught when Constance enquired about her father's account at the store, and her curiosity was such that she was compelled to speak.

"I do beg your pardon for my seeming rudeness," the woman said. "But I couldn't help overhearing the name of Clifford Seaforth. Is it possible that you are the daughter of the Marquess of Wrightwood?"

Constance quickly appraised the woman before responding. She was of a comfortable age, her hair tipped with silver in front and shading to a soft brown in the back. Her eyes were kindly and her smile infectious.

"Yes, I am Constance Seaforth. Forgive me. Have we met?"

"No, my dear, but I was well acquainted with your father before he left for Cornwall and rented The Beeches out to the Swedish ambassador's aide." She shook her head. "Clifford was such a charmer. I heard that he passed on a few years ago. Such a loss." She touched Constance's arm with her gloved hand. "Please accept my belated condolences."

"Thank you. We are just now getting settled at The Beeches. Aunt Millicent and I have only recently returned here from Cornwall, where we have been residing for several years."

The woman fished in her reticule and offered her card. "My name is Emmeline Chambers. The Countess of Smithfield."

Constance acknowledged the introduction and extended the courtesy to her Aunt Millicent.

Lady Smithfield clasped her hands together. "I would be so pleased if the two of you would join me for tea this afternoon at my home. We'll be quite alone and I would so love to talk to you again about your dear father." She patted her hair in an unconscious gesture. "I know this is short notice, but do please say you will."

Constance looked questioningly at Aunt Millicent, who spoke. "Very kind of you, I'm sure. Yes, my niece and I will be delighted to have tea with you."

"Lovely. The address is on the card. I'll see you later this afternoon," she said, waving goodbye.

Constance arranged for the fabric to be cut and delivered. The rest of their shopping had to wait for another day in order to allow them enough time to get ready for tea at the home of the Countess of Smithfield. It took every minute of the remaining time to sort out what they were going to wear.

The house was a respectable Mayfair mansion with carefully manicured grounds and buildings in a fine state of repair. Lady Smithfield greeted them with less exuberance than she had demonstrated earlier that afternoon. A yapping puppy chased at her heels, but she seemed oblivious.

"My dears," she said, extending her hands. "You will think me most ungracious, but there is a small emergency below-stairs to which I must attend at once. Would you be so generous as to excuse me for perhaps ten minutes?"

"Please take your time," Millicent said. "We shall be quite comfortable here."

The countess smiled her gratitude and said the butler would serve tea shortly.

Constance and Millicent seated themselves and quietly discussed the various objets d'art that had been placed about the room. Constance particularly enjoyed the paintings. Millicent fell in love with an ancient Greek vase that featured a relief of Eos sprinkling the earth with dew.

Ten minutes drifted into fifteen. Constance, intrigued by the scruffy puppy that had fallen asleep with a rag doll between its paws, took out her small drawing pad and began to sketch it.

Millicent was entranced. "What a talent you have, child. I like this better than some of those funny faces you draw."

Constance laughed. "What limited talent I do have lies in caricatures, Aunt Millicent. We both know I'll never be an accomplished artist."

"Practice, my dear. In a few days your little studio will be finished and you will have the perfect place to draw."

Just then Lady Smithfield returned. "Here I am at last. I trust Mason has taken good care of you." She offered to refresh their tea, then poured a cup for herself.

"What is this? Do we have an artist in our midst?" She picked up the sketch pad and studied it critically. "Why, this is my little Moppett. How wonderfully charming. I wonder, might I have this? I'm sure my husband would so like to have it framed for his study."

"I'm flattered that you want it. Of course you may keep it, Lady Smithfield."

She clasped it to her chest. "Tell me. Would the two of you do me the honour of attending a party I'm giving tomorrow evening at my home? Just a small party. I would so love to afford my friends an opportunity to meet you."

Constance glanced at Millicent, who nodded her agreement. They stayed for another half hour, then took their leave. The countess reminded them of the party before saying goodbye.

On the way back to The Beeches, Millicent could talk of nothing else but their good fortune. "Lady Smithfield is a very close friend of Lady Sefton, one of the seven women who control all of London society. A bid from her practically guarantees a membership in Almack's, and without that, my dear, one might as well forget the London Season and go back to the country."

"You do love parties, don't you, Aunt Millicent?"

"And why not? It's about the best place to find a husband."

Constance was shocked. "Truly! I didn't have the least idea you were husband hunting, Aunt Millicent."

Millicent guffawed. "Good heavens, child! It's you, not I, whom I'm talking about, my girl. It's one thing for me to play the nun, but I'll not have you mooning around for lack of a man to warm your bed."

"Don't be ridiculous. I'm happy enough. I have no objection to being a spinster." But even as she said it Constance knew she was shading the truth every so slightly. There was still a remembered warmth in the pit of her stomach when she thought of Jeremy St.

James. If she closed her eyes this minute she knew she would call up the look of desire in his incredible indigo eyes, could feel those strong hands as they lifted her onto the chaise.

She pulled the strings of her reticule in frustration. Leave it to her to be attracted to a man of such ill repute. Fortunately they travelled in different circles. She wasn't likely to see him again. And that was for the best, wasn't it?

But that night when she was alone, Constance sat in bed with her sketchbook propped against her knees and began to draw his face.

CHAPTER FOUR

THE DAY OF THE Smithfield party began with a grey sky that darkened around midmorning and cloaked the gardens all afternoon in cool, misty rain. Lacey, the straw-haired young abigail who had been hired by the Stavers to look after Constance's and Millicent's wardrobes, complained uneasily.

"Not a good sign, ma'am. 'Tis sure to bode ill for the two of you iffen the sky don't clear soon. Rainyday parties is bad luck, me old mum always told me."

Millicent sniffed. "The bad luck will be yours, girl, if you don't do something decent with my hair."

Constance laughed. "You're just looking for a compliment, Aunt Millicent. Your hair looks lovely, as you well know."

Millicent patted the riot of soft strawberry-blond curls. "It'll do, I suppose." She turned her attention to Constance. "I see you decided on the blue taffeta. Good. It shows off your figgah to perfection. There ought to be one or two eligible men to take notice."

Constance studied her reflection and was dismayed at the décolletage. "It's a little too revealing. I'm going to wear the ivory lace shawl, as well."

"Indeed, you *are* becoming spinsterish. Never mind. Do as you please. It's time we were leaving, at any rate." She reached for her grey cloak.

"Why not wear the black velvet cape? It would be dashing with your silver lamé gown and that onyx-and-diamond necklace. You'll be the sensation of the party, Aunt Millicent."

"Tut-tut. You're just trying to make me feel good." She smiled broadly. "But it's quite exciting, isn't it, to be back in the social whirl? And it's stopped raining. That ought to make Lacey happy."

The town carriage smelled a bit musty after the rain but it didn't dampen their spirits. It occurred to Constance that they both sounded as giddy as a pair of debutantes out for their first soirée. Despite some indefinable misgivings, she was glad that they had left Cornwall to make their home in London. For her own part she particularly loved the proximity to the Royal Galleries and the wealth of daily newspapers that London had to offer. But more than her own pleasure, Constance was pleased to see her aunt blossoming in the social whirl of the London ton.

The carriage driver had to jockey for position in line with all the other carriages waiting to discharge passengers at the entrance to the Smithfield house. He leaned down and told them it would be only a few minutes until they could alight.

Constance looked around wide-eyed. "I thought she said a small party. I'd hate to attend a large one. There wouldn't be room to breathe."

"Don't complain. The more people there are here, the better chance you'll have at making a good match."

"Aunt Millicent!"

"Sorry, my pet. I'll try to behave myself," she said while at the same time smiling at everyone who nodded in their direction.

From the moment they entered the grand salon, the party was a blur of fashionable gowns, glittering jewels, dandies in the newly fashionable trousers, older men in satin knee breeches. Not all the faces were friendly when Lady Smithfield guided Constance and Millicent among the crowd and introduced them. The two women were scrutinized, mentally weighed and catalogued, depending on whether the party goers saw them as a threat, a source of gossip or people worth cultivating.

Constance was amazed at the number of young women whose mothers were obviously in the market for prospective sons-in-law who could afford to keep their daughters in a constantly pampered state. They took one look at Constance, recognized the fact that she was a little beyond the first blush of young womanhood, decided she was not, therefore, serious competition and welcomed her. Constance, certainly still a beauty but with a maturity that four-and-twenty could bring, was at first surprised, then amused.

When the incredible Seven were introduced, Millicent was in her glory. The seven women who ruled Almack's were Lady Cowper, young, beautiful and the most popular; Lady Jersey, who looked like a queen of tragedy in some travelling theatre group;

Lady Sefton, the kind and amiable friend of Lady Smithfield; Lady Castlereagh and Mrs. Drummond-Burrell, the grand dames; Princess Esterhazy, youngest of the seven; and Countess Lieven, the haughty one who hardly acknowledged the introduction.

It occurred to Constance that they were not all that different from many of the other bejewelled guests. She made an effort to speak with each one individually, except Countess Lieven, who gave her a curt nod and walked away.

Dinner was arranged in a long buffet. Its fourteen courses seemed to stretch on endlessly.

After dinner the men took themselves off to the gaming room to enjoy some spirits and tobacco. The women retired to the grand salon to gossip and refresh themselves. Constance was delighted to see that Millicent was enjoying herself.

For her own part she would have preferred to walk alone in the garden or browse among the beautiful paintings and family portraits that lined the wide gallery, but it simply wasn't done. Constance no longer saw strict adherence to the rules as something of major importance, but until she was better known, she must try to maintain the correct behavior.

Lady Smithfield found her studying a small watercolour by Elliott. "Lady Constance, I've been showing some of my friends the drawing you made of our Moppett. Would it be asking too much for you to do a little sketch or two while you are here?"

Constance laughed. "I'm not sure whether to be embarrassed or flattered, Lady Smithfield. The truth is I didn't bring my sketchbook."

"Oh, I'm certain we could find something suitable, if you are willing."

"Of course, providing you don't expect too much. I warned you that I am not a true artist."

Her hostess fetched a thick pad of fine-quality drawing paper and a selection of pencils and pens. In no time Constance was surrounded by a group of enthusiastic women. Earlier her eye had been entranced by a young debutante as she leaned over the stairway balustrade to talk to her beau at the foot of the stairs. A few tendrils of her lustrous black hair escaped as she reached down for a rose blossom her gentleman friend was handing to her.

Remembering the scene, Constance sketched an outline then began filling in the shadows and highlights with quick flicks of the pencil. The dark hair, the white gown, the small cupid's-bow mouth.

It was this last feature that clearly identified the person as Miss Penelope Dobbs-Rengstad, and the girl squealed when she saw it. "Is that me? Goodness, am I really that pretty?"

Constance stifled the urge to tell her no. Like many artists of the time, whenever she drew a woman's face she tried to romanticize it, make it prettier than it was. For wasn't it better to make someone feel good?

Other women were impressed by Constance's lightning-fast sketches and asked that their own likenesses be captured.

In what seemed only a few short minutes the men, lured by the laughter and frivolity, began drifting into the room. One callow youth pushed his way through the group of women and leaned over Constance's shoulder, a bit more intimately than she would have liked.

"I'll bet you can't draw men as well as you can draw women."

Constance lifted her head and studied him carefully. The room quieted. "Perhaps not. But I can draw boys. Would you care to pose for me?"

He grinned at being properly set down but proved to be a good sport. "Right now? Should I take off my clothes?" he quipped.

"Whichever is more natural for you."

The guests laughed and crowded closer. The young buck struck a pose that vaguely resembled a statue of a famous general.

"Very good. Now stand still," Constance said.

The conversations slowly died as the drawing began to take shape. Since Constance sat with her back near the wall, only a few people were aware of how the picture progressed.

"Does it look like me?" The young man asked, his impatience beginning to show.

Constance drew several quick lines, grandly exaggerating her subject's petulant lower lip. A few more lines over emphasized his rather close-set eyes.

The woman behind Constance laughed. "I say, Bertie, it does look like you. She's caught more than your look, she's seen right inside you."

Constance signed her name with a flourish and handed the caricature to the young man.

He blustered in surprise. "What ho? This is me all right, but you've drawn me as a tyke in grown-up clothes."

The crowd burst into laughter. One man grabbed the youth around the shoulders. "Now that's our Bertie as we all know him. A little boy pretending to be a man."

They wanted more. So Constance drew four or five more sketches, until at last she was tired. She stood. "Thank you for being so kind but I think perhaps I'll rest for—"

Before she could say more, someone had grabbed her arms in a firm grip. Her captor stood behind her, and he leaned down to speak in her ear.

"Come with me and don't make a scene or I'll drag you out of here by your hair."

Before she knew what was happening she was hauled out of the room and into a small corridor that led through a side door into the conservatory.

"Just what the devil do you think you are doing here?" the voice growled. Then she was whirled around to face the speaker.

"You! Lord Jeremy," she gasped. "What are you doing here?"

"I happen to be a guest in this house. Now answer my question. How did the likes of you happen to find employment as an entertainer in a house like this?" His indigo eyes blazed. "I thought your talents were of the more physical variety."

"How dare you speak to me like that? Take your hands off me, you miserable oaf."

"Not until you've apologized to Her Ladyship for pushing in where you don't belong."

"I'll do no such thing."

His eyes blazed. "Have you lost your senses? Come with me now before it's too late. My offer stands. I am still willing to be your protector."

"I'd rather die first."

"Then the least you can do is to take your leave before someone recognizes you and makes Her Ladyship into a laughingstock."

Constance pushed his hands away from her. "The only one likely to be a laughingstock is you, my lord. Now get out of my way before my companion comes looking for me."

He swore competently. "So you are determined to continue this charade?"

Constance smiled despite the fact that she was visibly shaking. "Charade? My lord, how amusing that you, of all people, could object to a charade when you have spent your whole life masquerading as a gentleman."

Too late, Constance realized she had gone too far. His eyes changed from indigo to a dark purple blue and his mouth whitened around the edges of his moustache.

He felt the swift passage of blood through his veins as he confronted her, barely able to keep from taking her then and there. He knew she was baiting him. Knew that she enjoyed seeing his rage that was part anger—but more than a little physical desire.

The taffeta dress moulded to her body like blue ice. It caught the light in just the right places to make a man want to caress and hold her. The ivory lace shawl neither concealed nor revealed but seemed a deliberate, calculated attempt to intrigue a man's curiosity to explore further.

His voice was deadly. "So you think I am less than a gentleman, eh? Well, why don't we just find out, since I've already nothing to lose in your eyes."

He pulled her to him and kissed her. Constance struggled against him, but he was too strong for her. At last she permitted herself to go limp in his arms. The kiss gentled and for the briefest instant she responded before common sense took over and she broke from his arms.

At that moment Lady Smithfield opened the door to the conservatory and stepped in, closing the door behind her.

"Lady Constance? Is that you? Are you all right, my dear?"

Constance settled her gown back into place. "Yes, yes, I'm quite all right. If you'll excuse me, Lady Smithfield, I'm still not quite rested from my journey. Aunt Millicent and I will take our leave now."

"But of course, my dear. May I see you to the cloakroom or would you prefer to be alone?"

"Thank you. I can manage."

"Very well. We'll discuss this tomorrow." Her meaning was not well hidden.

Constance murmured something that indicated neither agreement nor dissent, then escaped into the corridor to the drawing room as if she were being pursued.

In the conservatory, Lady Smithfield turned to the earl and drew herself up to her full height. "And now, my dear Jeremy, would you be so kind as to tell me what is going on between the two of you? Lady Constance looked as if she were under attack.''

"*Lady* Constance?" The question came from a sudden hollow spot far down in the pit of his stomach.

"Yes," she said mildly. "Or do you have another of your women hidden behind the ferns in the conservatory?"

"Your Ladyship, forgive me, but this is no time for humour. The woman who was just in here...what is her name?"

Lady Smithfield smiled. "Oh, Jeremy! Don't be such a tease. Even you wouldn't be caught in an embrace with a woman you've never met."

"I've met her, ma'am. I simply don't know her name."

Lady Smithfield looked startled. "Indeed. I'm beginning to believe you. Why, she's Lady Constance Seaforth, daughter of the late Marquess of Wrightwood."

"Are you quite certain?"

"Jeremy, don't be absurd. I've known her father for years. Quite well, in fact. And Constance is the very picture of him. Such a man he was!"

Jeremy leaned against the wall and groaned. "Dear God. I've made a complete jackass of myself."

"It's hardly the first time, my boy. I remember how smitten you were with your French teacher. You were truly convinced she'd marry you, and as I recall, you gave us quite a time."

"I was sixteen, Lady Smithfield. This is rather different. And, dash it all, there are still a number of things left unexplained. Maybe you can tell me."

Lady Smithfield shrugged. "I don't have any answers. You'd best go to her. That's what you want to do, anyway, isn't it?" She brushed away his protest. "Don't bother to answer. I can tell by the feverish look in your eyes that you've more than questions on your mind. As for me, I must get back to my guests."

"No!" Jeremy put out his hand to stop her. She looked down at it, then up at him in an unspoken reprimand. He took his hand away.

"Just this, please, Your Ladyship. Can you tell me where to find her? Where does she live?"

She hesitated, weighing the alternatives. "Suffice it to say that you would doubtless find out from someone else, so I suppose I may as well tell you. She's moved back into the family home on Mount Street— the one that was rented by the Swedish ambassador's aide and his family. It's called The Beeches."

She put her hand on his arm. "Jeremy, you know I care for you and think highly of you, despite your somewhat unsavory reputation. But be careful with this young woman. She's not one of your giddy society debutantes. There's much more to her than that, and I would be loath to see her get hurt."

Jeremy bowed and kissed her hand. "I respect your opinion, Lady Smithfield, though I'm afraid a monstrous bit of damage has already been done. I'll do my best to make amends."

CONSTANCE WAS STILL in a state of nerves when she arrived home and reached the safety of her bedroom. Millicent had been miffed by their sudden departure, but when Constance explained that she had had a confrontation with Jeremy St. James, Millicent was contrite. Nothing was more important to her than her niece's state of mind.

"Would you like me to sit with you for a while, my dear?"

"No. It isn't necessary. I'm more angry than anything."

"A shame. And it started out to be such a lovely party."

Constance unfastened the combs from her hair and let it spill over her shoulders. "I'm sorry to spoil it for you, Aunt Millicent. You seemed to be having a pleasant chat with a certain older gentleman."

"Indeed. He was not all that old."

"I didn't mean that he was. Has he asked to, er, pay you a call?"

"What rot. Of course not. We...we have mutual friends."

"May I ask who?"

"You may not." She yawned openly. "Truth is I'm more tired than I thought. If you'll excuse me, child, I think I shall retire."

They said their good-nights and Constance closed the bedroom door. Millicent had already drawn the heavy draperies against the night vapours. She firmly believed that fresh air contaminated the lungs. For months now, Constance had waited until her aunt had gone to bed before she flung open the curtains to the night sky. In another quick move she unlatched the casement windows and breathed deeply of the rain-freshened air.

But the air didn't give her the feeling of contentment that she had expected. Try as she might, Constance could not shake the dull pain that settled in her chest after her scene with the Earl of Marshfield. Why, why did he have to come back into her life? She was so sure she had seen the last of him on the morning that she left The Tart Shoppe.

Her heart contracted. Ill-tempered as he was, it would be just like him to spread the word about where he had met her. That would certainly make short work of her successful introduction to Polite Society. What did it matter to the gossips if he had visited The Tart Shoppe with far less honorable intentions?

She swore softly, then out of guilt looked over her shoulder to be sure Aunt Millicent hadn't heard. "Why do I let him bedevil me this way?"

She lay in bed and considered the question from all sides before coming to the logical, though less than satisfactory conclusion. "Why not?" she again wondered aloud. "If I had another man in my life, Jeremy St. James would cease to be a problem."

Surely there was some other man with eyes that could bury themselves in your soul. Before Jeremy intruded on the scene that evening, she'd had a goodly number of men fawning over her. Why not live a little before she settled into her dotage? Millicent would certainly approve.

After all, she had the money, she had the position, and her face and figure, she knew, were not without appeal. She rolled onto her side and began planning. Parties. What fun she could have giving a garden party on the spacious terrace. There were so many people she could invite, and Lady Smithfield would surely help. The ideas tumbled through her head. . . .

At first she thought it was the pounding of her heart, she heard, but it proved to be someone hammering on the front door. Alarmed, Constance reached for her dressing gown and slippers and crept downstairs. The butler had also wakened. Stavers, his hair standing in silver spikes on the top of his head, somehow managed to look dignified in his ancient dressing gown. He opened the peephole in the door and asked the caller to speak.

Constance was unable to hear what the caller said, but Stavers answered, "Her Ladyship has already retired, sir. Would you be so kind as to leave your card?"

Constance touched the butler's arm. "Who is it, Stavers?"

"'Tis Jeremy St. James, I believe. He's most insistent, my lady. I doubt that he's in his cups, but he does seem most overwrought and must unwilling to leave."

"It's all right, Stavers. I'll speak to him."

"Would you like me to get a pistol, my lady, just in case?"

"I don't think that will be necessary." She suddenly remembered. "Oh. I left my reticule at the party. He's probably come to return it to me."

"Yes, my lady."

Stavers unlocked the door and stood aside with all the dignity of an officer in full-dress uniform. Jeremy brushed by him with a curt nod.

"Lady Constance, I—"

Constance was in no mood for another confrontation. "Just leave it on the table and go."

"I . . . what?"

"My reticule. You brought it to me, didn't you? Isn't that why you've come?"

"No." He glanced over at Stavers, who calmly stood his ground. "I came to apologize. I made a complete and utter fool of myself. Not just tonight, but—"

"Indeed. I perceive that wasn't too difficult. You've had a great deal of practice, so I've heard."

Stavers snickered, then coughed discreetly.

Jeremy looked irritated. "Isn't there some place we could be alone?"

"Surely you jest, my lord? The last time we were alone you took what you wanted without so much as a by-your-leave. I shudder to think what fate might have held in store had Lady Smithfield not appeared in the nick of time tonight."

Jeremy pulled at his snowy cravat, which seemed to be cutting off his wind.

"You're enjoying seeing me grovel, aren't you, Lady Constance?"

"Grovel? You haven't begun to grovel, Lord Jeremy. If I had my way you would be chased starkers down Fleet Street for the gross indignities you would have sought to prevail upon me."

He looked shocked. "But I thought you were . . . er . . ."

"Don't say it. I know what you thought. It doesn't change my opinion, however."

His gaze darkened, and even in the flickering glow from the gas torchlight, Constance felt the incredible seduction deep in those indigo eyes.

CHAPTER FIVE

HIS GAZE CONTINUED to hold her. Constance felt herself being drawn into it as if she were under a hypnotic spell. She pulled her dressing gown close under her chin. "I think perhaps you had better leave, my lord. I deem it highly improper for a gentleman to call on a lady at this time of night."

She looked at him through lowered lashes and added, "Of course you are quite accustomed to nocturnal visits, as I recall, considering our original encounter."

He swore softly. "What must I do to make amends?"

"Why, nothing at all. It's not me to whom you owe an apology. You were not required to pay for *my* time."

"Very well, then, no apology is offered you. I trust that you will bear no hostility should I happen to leave my card and ask to be permitted to call on you?"

"Oh, I wouldn't go as far as to say that!"

She glanced quickly over at Stavers, whose eyes held an unmistakable twinkle. Lord Jeremy noticed it, too. He stroked his moustache.

"I give you my word, Lady Constance, that I will call at a more suitable hour. Perhaps we could take the air in Green Park."

He thought he saw a spark of interest, but her answer left much to be desired.

"Leave your card if you wish. I guarantee you nothing, however."

He laced his hands behind his back and stood firm. "Or perhaps we could visit the Royal Academy. The gallery is once again exhibiting the fine paintings by Joseph Mallord William Turner."

She caught her breath. "Oh, could we?" Too late, she realized how eager her voice had sounded.

"Tomorrow at three."

"I have engagements tomorrow and Monday. Could we say Tuesday?"

"If that is your wish."

"Yes. Yes. I think... I think it would be better a few days hence."

Jeremy bowed. "It seems an eternity away, but I shall call for you at three on Tuesday."

"I... Aunt Millicent and I will look forward to it."

He grinned. "Ah, yes. We must not forget your chaperon. Until then, I bid you good-night."

Later, when Constance had returned to her bedchamber, she lay abed and studied the lace trim on the canopy of her four-poster. He was extremely adroit, that man. How easily he was able to manoeuvre her into a position where she had forgotten her anger and accepted his invitation. But surely he must realize it was the paintings she looked forward to seeing and not himself.

A nagging doubt took root before she was able to fall asleep. If it really were the paintings she wanted to see, why was it necessary to have Lord Jeremy as an escort? Seeing him publicly would serve only to feed the gossip mongers. And then it might be only a question of time until word got out about her overnight sojourn at The Tart Shoppe. It would ruin both her and Aunt Millicent socially. But what was she to do?

Constance was plagued with uncertainty. She would have to tell the earl that she had changed her mind. One thing was certain—Aunt Millicent was happier now than Constance had ever seen her. That meant more to Constance than the mere question of punctiliousness, but it would be less than expedient to chance stirring up rumours so soon after their entrance into society. She made a mental note to send a messenger with their regrets to Jeremy St. James no later than Monday afternoon.

On Tuesday the ormulu clock had barely struck the hour of three when Constance heard a carriage drive up. Parting the window curtain in her private sitting room, she looked down just in time to see Jeremy St. James alight from a smart open carriage and, slapping his gloves across a muscular thigh, walk briskly toward her front door.

Constance gasped. "Aunt Millicent! Aunt Millicent, come quickly."

Millicent rushed in from her nearby bedroom, where she was tatting a new trim for her fichu.

"What? Dear heaven, what is it, Constance?"

"Lord Jeremy has just arrived."

"In truth? I thought you sent a message declining his invitation."

"I did, but something must have gone awry. Hurry. We must make ourselves decent."

Moments later, Stavers delivered the earl's card on a silver salver. Constance told the butler to make him comfortable and inform him they would be down directly.

It was a short fifteen minutes later when they at last considered themselves presentable.

Jeremy rose as the two women entered. Seeing how well turned out they were, he was more certain than ever that he had not been mistaken. They had no legitimate reason for sending their regrets. Lady Constance might be clever in her concerted effort to play the reluctant maiden, but not as clever as he was in his determination to court her.

He bowed from the waist and made a great show of presenting a bouquet of primroses to the elder lady.

"May I say the two of you are looking especially lovely. The weather is perfect for our ride in my phaeton and a visit to the Royal Academy."

There was little doubt that Constance's curtsey lacked its usual grace. Jeremy was highly amused by her expression of absolute consternation.

"My lord, this is most awkward. Yesterday morning I sent a message to your house that my aunt and I would be indisposed."

"I say now. Isn't that strange? Are you certain the message was delivered to the right house?"

"Yes, of course. I sent one of my own servants, a local boy who knows his way about town. There could be no mistake."

He stroked his moustache. "A confounded embarrassment, I'd say. Do forgive me. It was not my intention to intrude." He looked over at Millicent, who studied him with levelled gaze. She was not one to be easily fooled, but Lady Constance, less keen of eye at this precise moment, was entirely sympathetic.

"Please do not apologize, my lord. Suffice it to say that you are here now. Perhaps Aunt Millicent and I could manage to be ready in a few minutes if you still wish to keep the appointment."

He bowed. "Nothing would give me more pleasure, but if it is to be an inconven—"

Constance interrupted. "No. Not at all. Do sit down and take your leisure while we get ready."

She was not to get off so easily. He contrived to sound generous. "In truth, Lady Constance, I don't see how I can ask you to accompany me when you so obviously prefer to spend the afternoon at home."

She clasped her hands together in front of her. Her voice rose a notch or two. "On the contrary. I'm sure the misunderstanding is entirely my fault." He could see that she was thoroughly unsettled as she continued, "I must have a word with young Michaels. As for this afternoon, if you can be patient, Aunt Millicent and I will not keep you waiting overlong."

Behind Lady Constance's back, Millicent flashed him a secret smile, which spoke more than the words that they had so carefully exchanged.

So he was right after all, the earl thought. The note, which had indeed been delivered the day before, had been a whim of the moment, a weak attempt by Lady Constance to postpone their meeting. Instinct told him that she had wanted to see him all along. Was it her pride or a lack of trust that made her decide to keep her distance? Whatever her motive, he counted it a significant victory that he had outsmarted her.

The women were ready in record time. Constance wore one of her nicer ensembles, a moss-green velvet with tiny pearls sewn into the seams of the bodice. She told herself she was dressing to lift her spirits and not to impress Jeremy St. James. Millicent teased her about it, but then, Millicent was always looking for a bit of intrigue where none existed.

Constance had mixed emotions about spending the afternoon with His Lordship. Part of her was over-joyed at the prospect of getting to know his better side, if indeed one existed, but a wiser part told her that she was a fool to play his game.

To her surprise the afternoon passed quickly and without untoward incident. Constance was impressed by his knowledge of the art world. She was privately delighted to know that he liked Turner's work as much as she did.

While Millicent was looking at a display of small paintings by the Swiss artist Fuseli, Jeremy cupped Constance's elbow in his hand and directed her toward an alcove where a large oil painting stood alone. It depicted Hannibal crossing the Alps in a snow-storm.

Constance put her hands to her face. "Oh! How magnificent. Such power. You can almost feel the storm building."

"Turner is a master at painting the elements. At Devonshire he has been known to take his sketch-book and go out in a fishing boat in the foulest of weather in order to record his impressions first-hand."

"His dedication shows. I think perhaps he is my favourite painter."

"Then you shall have to meet him. He has a house on Queen Anne Street where he exhibits his paint-ings, even though he has complete access to the Royal Academy."

"Truly, would it be possible?"

Jeremy laughed. "Anything is possible if one is de-termined."

"Would that it were true!"

"Trust me, Lady Constance." His moustache twitched. "Tell me what it is you want and I will see that it comes to pass."

"Spoken like a man who is used to having his own way." Her smile took the sting out of her words. "You are more than generous, my lord, but I find little that I want. I have my house, more friends than I can count, the freedom to come and go as I please—within reason." She spread her hands. "I am a truly fortu-nate woman."

He folded his arms and leaned against the wall to more fully study her. "Yes. You have the look of a woman who is nearly content with her lot in life."

"Only nearly?"

"Hmm. Yes. Sometimes when you think no one is looking, I see a certain sadness creep into your eyes."

Constance pulled her gaze away from his. "What utter rubbish. You, sir, have a vivid imagination."

"No. I speak the truth, whether you choose to admit it or not."

"Perhaps you see what you want to see, my lord. You would like to believe that because I'm a woman without a man to protect me I must necessarily be unhappy."

"Those are your words, my lady, not mine. But speaking of what *I* want . . . it would please me no end if you would attend a gala with me tomorrow night at Vauxhall Gardens. The Gardens are not what they used to be, mind, but there is to be a concert, I believe."

"Thank you, but Aunt Millicent and I are joining a group of friends at Almack's."

"Would it be presumptuous of me to ask whom?"

Her cheeks dimpled. "You may ask, but I have no intention of telling you. Suffice it to say that I have been invited to join a small gathering for the purpose of making new friends."

He raised his eyes to the ceiling. "Almack's, the temple of the ton, will be a deadly bore. They serve weak lemonade and tea and offer nothing but bread and butter and rounds of cake so stale one could use them for cart wheels. And it will be a crush. There are no small gatherings at Almack's.

"Besides," he continued, "I thought you had met everyone who amounted to anything. I'm told that you've been invited out every night since you arrived and that you are much in demand—'' his eyes sparkled with mischief ''—for one who has managed to stay unwed somewhat beyond the first blush of maidenhood.''

She glared at him. ''I think it's safe to say that there are a few people I have yet to meet. The Prince Regent, for one, and the Princess Caroline.''

''You set your sights high. When would you like to meet them?''

She waved her hand airily. ''Oh, any afternoon would be fine. Just ask the Prince to send his card around and I shall endeavour to save at least a little bit of time for him.''

''How generous of you,'' he said dryly. ''Better still, I'll see that you are included on his guest list. He is an extravagant host, as you may have heard.''

''If half the stories that are being circulated are true, he would have to be outrageous as well as unscrupulous.'' She seated herself on a viewing bench and looked up at Jeremy, who regarded her with amusement.

''Be assured, Lady Constance, that the Prince of Wales is a far better man than some care to admit, and far worse than others could possibly realize.''

''Do you truly know him? I mean, to actually converse with him?''

''We have been known to exchange words on a number of occasions. The Regent does not agree with many of my views, but one might say we are casual friends.''

''Then you are one among few. His extravagance has cost him a great deal of respect.''

"But his generosity on certain occasions has endeared him to others."

Constance, seeing Millicent approach, stood up. "Needless to say, my lord, you are a product of the city. Believe me, the farmers do not share your gentle feelings."

"Nor do you, I surmise. But in truth, you know little of my feelings. I'm curious, though. If you dislike his style, why then do you still wish to meet the Prince Regent?"

Constance looked shocked. "Why? Because he will one day be King when his father is no longer with us. That in itself should be reason enough. Do you not agree?"

He smiled. "I suppose I must. If for no other reason than to keep the peace."

Millicent overheard this last exchange and clucked her tongue. "Have you two been quarrelling again?"

"On the contrary, Miss Seaforth. Lady Constance and I have just discovered we have many interests in common."

He gave Millicent a conspiratorial look that took Constance by surprise. The two of them liked each other. How did it happen that Jeremy St. James was able to charm her aunt so quickly when Millicent knew full well his reputation as a rake and rogue of the first water? Millicent was no fleabrain. She was not easily taken in by fast-talking charmers. Constance secured a curl underneath the feathers of her hat. If she and her aunt were not constantly on their guard, Jeremy St. James could easily prove to be a liability, if not indeed a most dangerous man.

Their life in Cornwall had revolved around quiet walks among the heather on the headlands, riding down to the beach to watch the villagers net pilchard and overseeing the servants in the performance of their duties. London, during the Season, however was like another world. Hardly a day went by without some manner of fête or soirée. And between such gatherings, callers, at the appointed times, kept up a steady parade at The Beeches.

It was the Misses Amelia and Emily Parkhurst who had invited Constance and her aunt to join them at Almack's. They were most eager for Constance to meet a certain Lady Francine Stropshire, who until now had been visiting friends in the south.

"I know she will find you most interesting," Miss Amelia had told her several times. Why that might be, Constance was not quite sure, but she was curious. Besides, despite Lord Jeremy's warning that Almack's would be boring, Constance had enjoyed it during her one evening there, more for the social interchange than the exceedingly awful refreshments.

As usual on a Wednesday night, Almack's was crowded. King Street, just off St. James Street, had seen a veritable crush of carriages in all shapes and forms. Inside the assembly rooms, the musicians in the gallery were playing a dreary ballad that allowed for easy conversation. It was the best that could be said for them.

Amelia and Emily Parkhurst were all adither as they gathered a group of regulars around them in a small drawing room just off the ballroom. It was so filled with guests that there was room for only a few chairs. The Parkhurst party managed to acquire those while the others stood around them, pretending not to listen to the conversation.

A short time after they were settled, Emily Parkhurst jumped up. "Ah, here she is now," she said, a wide smile of triumph lighting her face when she saw a singularly striking woman making her way through the crush. "Over here, Francine, my dear. We've saved a place for you."

The women greeted each other, then Lady Francine seated herself between the sisters while Miss Emily performed the introductions. Constance and Lady Francine exchanged courteous, if cool, acknowledgements.

Miss Amelia clasped her hands in delight. "Well, here we are at last. I've so wanted the two of you to meet. You have so much in common."

Constance pondered what that could possibly be. Tiny, yet elegant, Lady Francine Stropshire was the epitome of a highly bred, young society woman who might well have been the hit of the previous year's debutante ball. Rubies and diamonds glittered on her small hands and were sprinkled lavishly in her extravagantly dressed blue-black hair.

For a few minutes they made an attempt at light conversation. It wasn't easy. *I don't like her,* Constance thought, and then wondered why. She knew it wasn't the woman's beauty that disturbed her. It had more to do with her bearing, a certain condescension that was too intangible to pinpoint.

A sudden commotion was taking place near the door to the ballroom. Constance was tall enough to see that it was Jeremy St. James who had entered. He caught her glance and sketched a mock salute, then started toward her, only to be stopped by the mass of people, most of whom had a word or two to say to him.

Constance managed to drag her attention back to the circle. It seemed to her that nearly half of the room was hanging on their words. Knowing as little as she did about Lady Francine, Constance tried to make up for it with an interested smile. "I'm sure you enjoyed the scenery as you travelled, Lady Francine. The south country is so beautiful this time of year."

Lady Francine folded her fan and let it fall to her lap. "It might have been if the farmers weren't creating such a rabble. Our coach was constantly being assaulted by stones and the most unimaginable filth." She picked up her fan and fluttered it quickly in front of her face. "Do you know they have the nerve to stand with their children right in the middle of the road and beg food from us? Some even went so far as to threaten us."

There was a murmur of sympathy from the listeners.

Constance refused to let it pass. "I suppose one can hardly blame them for begging if they are starving."

"Then let them grow crops," Lady Francine snapped.

"I doubt that a farmer would let his children starve if he had a choice. It's the small landowners whose plots are too small to grow wheat who are starving."

Constance ignored a look from Aunt Millicent, who stood off to the side, silently frowning as Constance continued.

"Don't you see? It's thanks to the Corn Laws that the farmers are losing their lands. They have to work either in the factories or in the mines to keep bread on the table. The north-country people manage, but there is no work to be had in the south."

Lady Francine laughed. "Then they should move to the north, wouldn't you agree?"

Miss Emily, apparently trying to smooth over the situation, spoke up. "I say, do let's talk of something else. Poverty is so boring."

There was a momentary babble of voices, and Constance forced herself to relax. She was, after all, a guest of the Parkhurst sisters. Why not try to keep the peace? During the next lull in the conversation she spoke up. "I've heard, Lady Francine, that you are very accomplished at the pianoforte. Have you studied long?"

Lady Francine's eyes were as cold as ice. "As with everything, it comes to a question of breeding, I suppose. My mother, as well as her father and his father before him, were trained musicians. I presume you do not play?"

Miss Emily laughed and Constance wondered if it were in response to the crudely veiled cut or from a case of nerves. To her credit, Miss Emily made an effort to cover her gaffe.

"Lady Constance is a fine artist. You must prevail upon her to do a sketch of you, Francine." She patted the young woman's hand and looked expectantly at Constance.

"Please don't confuse my simple drawings with fine art, Miss Emily. After viewing the Turner exhibit at the Royal Academy, I count my talent as less than nil."

Miss Amelia leaned forward and suddenly the room became very quiet. "The Turner exhibit?" she enquired. "I've been so wanting to see it, but I thought it was removed to Turner's home on Queen Anne Street some two weeks ago."

Constance warmed to the subject. "No indeed. We saw it only yesterday. Isn't that correct, Lord Jeremy?"

There was dead silence. In a room that was crowded to near capacity, it seemed not a soul breathed. Finally, Jeremy stepped forward. Constance wondered if she were the only one to notice the strained look on his face.

"Quite true, Lady Constance. I believe it is to remain another month."

He turned and made the semblance of a bow. "Lady Francine, how nice to see you. I wasn't aware you had returned."

The room appeared to wait for him to continue, or for Lady Francine to return the courtesy, but it was left to Jeremy to break the silence. "It was my impression that you were to be gone at least another week."

She regarded him with cool amusement. "It appears I returned none too soon, Jeremy, my dear. What is it they say? 'When the cat's away...'"

The room exploded in laughter. Too late, Constance realized that she had been deliberately set up by the Misses Emily and Amelia. She felt her face begin to burn. Jeremy looked stricken. For once he was caught with his mouth open and nothing to say.

Constance had plenty to say, but the time was not now.

Damn him! Damn him to destruction, she thought, as tears burned at the back of her eyes.

CHAPTER SIX

IT WAS THANKS to Lady Smithfield that Constance was able to make a graceful, if strategic, exit from the gathering. Lord Jeremy's expression had been, to say the least, unsettled when Constance met his gaze. He had resembled a small boy caught stealing sweets from the candy dish.

Before taking her leave, Constance had given him a look that might well have frosted a steaming tankard of rum. From all appearances, Jeremy had been about to speak to her, but all she could think about as she took her hasty, yet graceful, departure was the smug-faced Lady Francine and her sisterhood of plump little witches. Jeremy St. James was the last person on earth she wanted to talk to.

Paradoxically, Constance sat in her darkened bedchamber for several hours after the rest of the household had fallen asleep. It would have been so like the earl to come rapping on her door, creating all manner of fuss until she agreed to talk to him. Of course she would have ignored him. But when the clock had struck the hour of three and he still had not arrived, Constance finally convinced herself that he had gone instead to mend his fences with Lady Francine.

The morning sun had already burned the dew off the roses when Aunt Millicent marched into her room and began setting things right. "Get up, my girl. I can't have you acting the lie-abed with guests arriving in a few hours." She bustled about with all the energy of an innkeeper about to entertain royalty.

"Company?" Constance sat up, pulling off the nightcap and allowing her hair to mass around her shoulders. "I do hope you are funning me, Aunt Millicent."

"Have you forgotten today is our at-home day? We're sure to have a card or two, unless I miss my guess."

Constance groaned. "After last night? I don't think I want to see anyone, let alone show my own face in the daylight."

"Nonsense. We gave them something to talk about, that's all. It's a full measure better than being ignored. Where's your gumption, girl?"

Constance had to call up on all of her emotional reserves to get out of bed, get dressed and go downstairs. It seemed like no time before callers began to arrive.

Everyone, it appeared, had heard about the fiasco at Almack's the night before. Although no one came out and spoke directly about the circumstances of Constance's humiliation, the subject was always there, just below the surface. And Constance could feel them laughing.

Each time a carriage drove up in front, Constance forced herself not to run to the window. She would have been disappointed. Jeremy St. James was not among those who came to call.

Among the last to leave was Lady Smithfield. Constance knew that the woman had been watching her, and so she made every effort to keep a smile pasted on her face. When Millicent accompanied the Benthurst women to the door for a final goodbye, Lady Smithfield motioned Constance to sit next to her.

"Now then, Lady Constance, I want a word with you. I know how unsettled you are and I'm sorry. Someone should have warned you about Jeremy and his relationship to Francine."

Constance stiffened. "I doubt that anyone owed me an explanation. After all, Jeremy St. James is nothing to me."

"Indeed?" Lady Smithfield's look reflected her amusement. "If that is true, my friend, then you had best let your head know. For the past hour your eyes and ears have been tuned to the arrival of carriages. I suspect that whether you know it or not, Jeremy has made some sort of significant impression on you."

"He is a friend, nothing else."

"Then I assume you have no wish to know more about Lady Francine?" she said as she casually pleated the ribbons on her reticule.

"I . . . well, I . . ."

"I thought so. The truth of the matter is that the St. James and the Stropshire families have been neighbours for generations. Jeremy and Francine grew up together, so naturally there has been something of an unspoken agreement that eventually they would make the arrangements more personal."

She crossed, then uncrossed, her slim ankles in front of her. "Francine is a leaner. She's always looked to Jeremy to come to her aid, whether it's simply to fill a chair at the dining table or to see that she gets a coveted invitation to the Regent's ball."

"It was my impression that her hold on him went a little deeper than that."

"Oh, my dear, I do not mean to minimize the connection. There has been a great deal of pressure on him of late from both families for him to offer for her. After all, he can't expect her to wait much longer. It's a year—no, nearly two years—since her come-out. She's not getting any younger." Lady Smithfield apparently saw the expression on Constance's face and touched her hand. "Oh, my dear, I am so sorry. I truly did not stop to think that you are somewhat older than Francine."

"No apology is necessary. I have chosen not to marry because—"

"There is no need to explain. Suffice it to say that too much emphasis is placed on the need for a young woman to marry before the age of twenty. Why, indeed, should a woman have to marry at all, assuming she can provide for herself. Of course if one wishes to have children . . ."

Constance looked toward the window and tried without success to keep the wistfulness from her voice. "Yes. Therein lies the problem."

"Again I must apologize. It was not my intention to sadden you." She brightened. "I know what. Would you do me the honour of dining with me tonight at my home? I've been promising to show your dear aunt my collection of fans.''

"Could we make similar plans another time, Lady Smithfield? I feel a headache coming on."

"Nonsense. It's just this business of last night that's making you feel poorly. What you need is to get out."

"Truly, I don't want to be among people tonight."

"I swear to you, Constance, my dear. It will be just family. Now don't say no. I'll see you and Miss Seaforth promptly at seven."

Lady Smithfield took her leave before Constance could press her desire to postpone the engagement. Millicent was delighted by the invitation, but Constance, as she readied herself later, was uncomfortable for the first time with her approaching state of spinsterhood. She took special care with her dress, going so far as to add a touch of colour to her cheeks. It was a relief to be reminded that there were as yet no unsightly lines to mar her face. The lilac taffeta of her gown rustled comfortingly as she moved to the dressing table to select an amethyst pendant that had belonged to her mother. Its purplish fires, caught and surrounded by heavy gold filigree, danced in the lamplight, adding a welcome sparkle to her eyes. She had delayed so long that she had to rush to finish getting ready.

Lady Smithfield was too well schooled in the art of punctiliousness to comment on the Seaforth ladies' somewhat delayed arrival. Once the three women were settled in the library sipping tea from exquisitely thin Dresden cups, the conversation predictably drifted back to Lady Francine and Jeremy St. James.

Millicent enquired of Lady Smithfield, "If the families are so eager for the liaison, why does he not marry her? Lady Francine is certainly one of the most beautiful women I have ever seen."

"It is only on the surface, my dear Miss Seaforth. I grant you that Francine has all the graces of London's most popular debutante, but she is completely self-centred. As to why he doesn't offer for her, that, indeed, is the question. Suffice it to say that he doesn't want to."

Constance leaned forward to place her cup on the low, pink marble table. "Why should he marry and give up his free way of living? If truth be told, Lord Jeremy is not much better than Lady Francine when it comes to depth of character."

"On that I must disagree. Jeremy has changed of late. He is taking his duties seriously, attending meetings of Parliament, trying to keep up with and understand the needs of his estate, as well as the needs of the many poor unfortunates. You must take care not to underestimate him, Lady Constance. He has given up gambling and womanizing, though I suspect his reputation there was highly exaggerated."

Constance laughed sharply. "More likely underrated."

Her Ladyship smiled. "You're thinking of the incident at The Tart Shoppe."

Both Constance and Millicent paled. Millicent was the first to speak. "I...I don't quite know to what you might be referring."

Constance snapped. "Of course you do, Aunt Millicent. It is quite apparent that Lady Smithfield is privy to the latest on dit. Jeremy St. James mistook me for another type of woman and tried to buy me. It's as simple as that.''

Lady Smithfield was obviously shocked by Constance's lack of tact and was too stunned to speak.

Constance reached for her reticule and stood to take her leave rather than remain there to be insulted. "It is plain to see, Lady Smithfield, that you are exceedingly well informed for one who deigns to abhor gossip.''

There was a commotion at the door. Constance turned and paled as a familiar voice spoke. It was Lord Jeremy.

"And why wouldn't she be well informed? Lady Smithfield is my godmother and as close to me as my own mother.'' He bowed to the ladies and turned to smile at Lady Smithfield.

Constance refused to return his respects but stood fast, holding to the chair for support. "You, sir, are reprehensible! How could you be so insensitive as to defame my aunt and me to our friends? If indeed a friend she is!'' she stated, looking pointedly at Lady Smithfield.

Millicent was taken aback. "Constance! Do be still. You are speaking out of anger rather than good sense.''

"Outrage would be more appropriate. The nerve of some people to take an unfortunate incident and turn it into a tidbit for the gossip hens to pick at.''

Lady Smithfield rose. "I assure you, Lady Constance, that the story, what little I know of it, has not gone beyond these walls.'' She reached down and took

Millicent's hand. "Miss Seaforth, may I make so bold as to offer to show you the statuary you so much admired when you were last here last?"

"Oh my..." Millicent's gloved hand flew to her mouth. It was obvious she was torn between desire and duty. "I really should stay with Constance."

Jeremy folded his arms across his chest, a motion that emphasized his lean waist and muscular thighs, Constance noticed. She wondered how long he had practised in front of a mirror.

His voice was controlled but nevertheless reflected his amusement. "You needn't fear, Miss Seaforth. In no way shall I attempt to compromise your charge. Lady Constance is safe with me. Besides, what could harm her here?"

What indeed? Constance thought, but Millicent as always was taken in by Lord Jeremy's charm. It came as no surprise to Constance when her aunt dimpled up at him and excused herself "for just a few short minutes."

Constance turned and walked to the window, giving the earl the benefit of her back. "You are indeed running true to form, sir. I suppose you are telling everyone that you bedded me, as well as bartered for my favours. You know what this will do to my aunt and me? No self-respecting woman of the ton will even speak to us once they know we spent the night at The Tart Shoppe. Almack's will close its doors to us and no one will ever accept our cards."

He walked over to the window and took her by the shoulders, then turned her to face him. "It was you, my lady, who spoke out of turn. I only explained to my godmother how you became ill and chanced to arrive at The Tart Shoppe. We had words only about your illness. There was no intention of our ... unfortunate misadventure.''

Constance stared at him with her mouth open. "But Lady Smithfield said ... You said—''

"No, Lady Constance. It was your nimble mind creating gossip where there was none—until now. It was you and your quick tongue and sharp temper who let the mouse into the house, so to speak.''

Constance moved away from him and wilted into the nearest chair. "Oh, drat it all. Why couldn't I have kept still?''

"Why indeed? Now we both have some explaining to do to my godmother.''

She straightened and managed a reasonable glare. "It serves you right. If you had the decency not to patronize such a house of ill fame, none of this would have happened. I hope she disinherits you.''

"Not likely. She has a very high opinion of me.''

"Indeed! That makes two of you.''

"If your tongue were much sharper you could cut venison with it.''

"But I would first thrust it right between your shoulder blades,'' she said before she had time to think how her words might be misconstrued.

His eyes grew warm and a slow smile melted the sharp angles of his face. "I think I might like that.'' He studied her face. "Why are we quarrelling, Lady Constance?''

"Why? How dare you ask? You've done nothing but embarrass me since the moment I met you. You've taken two completely unblemished reputations and turned them into fodder for the gossip mongers to feast on."

"I thought we were getting on quite famously until last night. Truthfully now, didn't we enjoy our visit to the Royal Academy? Didn't we find dozens of things we hold in mutual concern? Didn't we enjoy one another's company?"

"Lay it to a temporary loss of sanity."

"On my part?" He grinned, obviously enjoying the game he was playing with words.

"The devil take you, Jeremy St. James."

"Admit it, Lady Constance. You are angry because I didn't tell you about Francine."

"What utter nonsense. I have nothing but pity for her. She is too...too..." To Constance's disgust, she began to stutter. For the life of her she couldn't think of a single set-down to describe the woman.

"Rich?" he asked. "Too beautiful, too well-bred? Is that the fault you find with her?"

"Of course not." She stabbed the air with her finger. "Too short! That's it. Lady Francine is far too short for one to hold any ill feelings toward her."

"Yes. I think you finally have it. She is a bit short. An extremely serious flaw, wouldn't you say?"

Constance knew he was laughing at her. Suddenly she realized how ridiculous it all was and she had to bend her head to hide her laughter.

He crossed to stand beside her. Leaning over, he lifted her chin in the palm of his hand. "I didn't tell you about Lady Francine because it didn't signify. She is not beholden to me, nor I to her."

She brushed his hand away. "My lord, you presume too much. Why are you telling me this?"

"Because you want to know. Because I want you to know."

"Toadflax! Your state of betrothal means not one whit to me."

"Then you are indeed a singular woman."

"Why do you say that?"

He plucked a pale rose from the vase and placed it in her hand. "There are few women of virtue who would consent to be courted by a man yet at the same time care nothing for the state of his betrothal."

"Courted by a man? Indeed!" Constance was so startled by his audacity that she punctured her finger on a thorn. She swore softly as blood seeped through the fabric of her lace glove. "Your imagination is remarkable, my lord, though your subtlety leaves something to be desired."

He pulled a square of snowy linen from his waistcoat and wrapped it around her finger. "Am I to understand that you have no desire to be courted?"

"No. Indeed I enjoy being courted. From the moment I arrived I have been courted by half a dozen eager young bucks. It does one good at my a—"

She had started to say age but caught herself in time. Or so she thought, until he grinned rakishly.

"At your age? Come now, Lady Constance. You are not *that* old. You are still young enough to dance to the tune and pay the piper, as well."

"But not nearly as young and pretty as Lady Francine."

"That is true."

She stood abruptly and glared at him. "Why, you inconsiderate oaf. I can't tell you how thoroughly I detest you."

"Perhaps you need practice. Would you care to try?" He reached into his waistcoat pocket. "As it happens, we have invitations to a ball, which I'm certain you'll not want to miss."

"I would advise you not to place too large a wager on it." She flung the rose in his face and it caught, tearing a slight scratch just below his eye. Small though it was, the blood oozed forth. He touched his hand to it.

"I was well aware, Lady Constance, that your rapier words could draw blood, but this is going a trifle too far. If you are quite finished with my handkerchief, perhaps we might stop the flow."

She caught her breath. "Oh, dear. I am so terribly sorry. I didn't mean to wound you. Is there something I can do?"

He smiled. "Think nothing of it." He took the handkerchief from her and dabbed at his face. "Of course, you owe it to me now to accept my invitation to the ball."

"I most certainly do not."

"As you wish. But your aunt will be disappointed. I'm quite sure she would be thrilled to join the Prince Regent and his party at Carlton House."

"You lie, my lord! You have no intention of taking me to the Regent's Ball."

"No? Would you care to place a wager?"

She chewed her lower lip in consternation. "Must you always try to best me?"

"Try? I thought I had."

"Careful, my lord. Next time you will suffer more than a prick from a thorn."

"At least there will be a next time. The ball is just over a week away. No doubt we'll see one another before then."

She eyed him warily. "If you are funning me about the invitation to Carlton House, I swear I will make you pay."

"If you will recall, I offered once to pay in gold coin, but you refused me."

Her face flamed. "Must you always twist my words? Please do me the courtesy of leaving before the others return."

He swept into a low bow. "Consider me gone. Until tomorrow, then." He gave her a quick salute, clicked the heels of his highly polished boots and left abruptly through a side door.

Constance put considerable effort into wiping the smile from her face before Lady Smithfield and Aunt Millicent returned to the salon.

Lady Smithfield looked around. "I say. Where has that incorrigible godson of mine gone to? Surely he hasn't left already."

"I'm afraid he has, and none too soon if I may say."

"Oh, Constance," Millicent wailed. "Surely you haven't argued again."

"Jeremy St. James and I do nothing *but* argue. He is an impossible man, completely void of conscience."

Lady Smithfield beamed. "He is a bit of a rake-hell, but undeniably charming, wouldn't you say?"

"I would not, though apparently my aunt doesn't agree with me."

Millicent blushed like a young girl. "Indeed! Ah, if only I were a few years younger..."

Lady Smithfield bobbed her head. "He does have that effect on women. Tell me, Lady Constance, are you seeing him again soon?"

Constance blushed. "As chance would have it, I am. But only out of—" She stopped. How could she explain that she had thrown a rose at him and wounded him?

"Out of...?" both women prompted.

Constance searched desperately for a word. "Out of...curiosity."

The women laughed heartily, then Lady Smithfield spoke. "My dear, you are the courageous one. Wasn't it curiosity that made Eve pluck the forbidden fruit?"

"Yes, my lady. But I have no intention of taking a bite."

They both looked at her without speaking. What was it she saw in their eyes? Envy? Pity? Sorrow for their lost youth? For a moment Constance was over-whelmed by the feeling that she was no longer in control of her future. That she was being caught up in a whirlwind too strong to resist.

It was only later, as Constance and Millicent pre-pared to leave the Smithfield home, that Constance realized her lace glove was missing. They searched the chair and the floor but there was no sign of it.

"It has to be here," Millicent said. "You haven't left the room since we arrived."

Lady Smithfield was upset. "What can I say, my dear? There is simply no sign of it."

Constance disliked all the fuss, especially after she recalled what in fact had happened to her glove. Jeremy, the cad, had taken it. How on earth was she to explain *that* choice bit of intrigue to her hostess without acting the part of a blushing maiden? Once again Jeremy St. James had succeeded in putting her at a decided disadvantage. One of these days she would gain the upper hand. And when she did... She smiled thinking how good it would feel to set him down properly, especially in front of a crowd of his admirers. He deserved it, didn't he? The thought was enough to allow her a good night's sleep.

CHAPTER SEVEN

CONSTANCE WAS CERTAIN that after the newness wore off, Polite Society would tire of inviting Millicent and her to their soirées, but it didn't happen that way. Even after the awful faux pas with Lady Francine, the invitations continued to pour in. A Spaniard of dubious intentions and a young lieutenant of the Royal Guard had been the most persistent of Constance's callers, but they held no interest for her.

She still had a great deal to learn about life in London, having been accustomed to the more flexible rules of country life in Cornwall. When she chanced to purchase a pair of brown kid boots, for instance, she was unaware how close she'd come to disaster. Fortunately, Lady Smithfield saw them before Constance appeared in public; otherwise, Constance would have learned the hard way that only tarts and light-skirts wore brown boots.

One lesson that held true for both town and country living was that gossip was the life's blood of conversation. And if that gossip proved to be about the favoured few, so much the better. The Earl of Marshfield and Lady Francine were certainly among the so ordained, and according to Aunt Millicent, Lady Constance was not far behind.

Although she had taken the liberty of exaggerating the truth to Lord Jeremy about her abundance of suitors, the lie soon became reality when calling cards, flowers, sweets and all manner of gifts began arriving at The Beeches. That Constance was unimpressed by any gentleman in particular made her suitors all the more persistent. Except Jeremy St. James. He was apparently content to wait out the flood of invitations, content in the knowledge that she would refuse all others in order to accompany him to the Regent's Ball.

Constance studied her reflection in the mirror. Was Jeremy merely content, or was he otherwise occupied? She hadn't seen him for days. Not at the Quales' musical evening, nor the Van Verdenmasters' garden party, nor even at Almack's, though if truth be told she had wearied of Almack's and spent little time there now.

Nor had she seen Lady Francine. The truth of the matter was obvious. "Toadflax!" she said aloud to no one in particular. The truth was all too apparent. No matter how Lord Jeremy tried to wiggle out of it, there was more to his relationship with Lady Francine than he chose to admit.

Lacey, the abigail who served both Constance and Millicent, walked into the bedchamber in time to see Constance stab her comb into her brush with more force than necessary.

"I warned ye, milady, not to mess wi' your hair. Now you've gone and drummed it up good."

"It does look a fright, doesn't it?" Constance said, discouraged with her aborted attempt to capture the latest style.

"Never you mind, Your Ladyship. I kin do it up fine iffen you would just sit still for a piece."

"I promise not to move."

Millicent came into the bedchamber at that moment. "Oh, yes indeed! Your new blue velvet is extremely becoming. I do wish I had your figure, girl. Old age wouldn't be so bad if one's shape didn't run to ruin."

"Don't be absurd. Your figure is excellent. Especially in that grey taffeta. The mulberry trim shows off your slim waist. It makes you look ten years younger."

"Would that it were true. If I don't stop going to parties I'll have to invest a fortune in corsets, as the Prince Regent does."

"Careful what you say, Aunt Millicent. Remember, we're to be his guests tonight at Carlton House."

"Pooh. The chances are he won't even be there. They say he often gives parties but stays sequestered in his private quarters."

"Even if the prince fails to join us at dinner we must give Jeremy credit for trying. He knows I would enjoy meeting the Regent but if need be, I will content myself with viewing the collection of oil paintings displayed at Carlton House."

"Speaking of Lord Jeremy... I came to give you a parcel that was just delivered by messenger."

Lacey threw down the comb and gave a sigh of exasperation. "Great lackaday! You might as well stop an' open it, milady. Ain't no way I can comb your hair an' you movin' around like a flea in a pot o' brandy.''

Constance didn't wait for the abigail to change her mind. She took the package, which was wrapped in thin silver paper and tied with a silver bow, through which was threaded a streamer of pink silk rosebuds.

"How did you know it was from Lord Jeremy?" Constance said, darting a quick look at her aunt.

"I read the card, of course. It bears the St. James crest." She handed it to Constance, who turned it over to display the coat of arms and his signature in fine script.

Only his name was signed. Jeremy St. James. She had hoped for something a little more... As soon as the word entered her thoughts she discarded it. "Romantic" was hardly a word she should apply to the exasperating earl. Even if he had declared his undying love she wouldn't have been satisfied. For one thing, she doubted that he knew the meaning of the word. But she would have settled for a message of sorts. Any message.

The paper concealed a narrow box. Inside was a layer of pink tissue, which she unfolded to reveal a pair of exceedingly fine lace gloves in the popular shade of eggshell white. Constance lifted them and slid one onto her hand.

"Have you ever seen anything so lovely, Aunt Millicent?"

"They must have cost him a fortune. I say, what an odd gift. Isn't there some meaning behind a gift of gloves?"

"'Ere now, there's somethin' else there under the wrap," Lacey said, leaning closer to get a good look. She scratched her head. "You can name it odd, all right. One glove? And not a proper match for the others."

Constance smiled, remembering the rose and the thorn. "It's not a gift, really. It's only a glove that I misplaced last week at the Smithfields'."

"It's not faithfulness," Aunt Millicent murmured.

"Whatever are you talking about?"

"The gloves, Constance. The gift of gloves." She struck her forehead with the flat of her palm. "Of course. It means that he's placing his life in the palms of your hands."

"What absolute drivel. You're as bad as Lacey with her omens and predictions. The gloves are simply a gift to make up for his ungentlemanly behaviour."

"I sincerely doubt that," Millicent stated. "Perhaps you should ask him. Or perhaps I should, since it is my duty to protect you from unseemly advances."

"You'll do no such thing, Aunt Millicent. The less said about this, the better. There are already too many tongues awagging among the haut ton. And that goes for you, too, Lacey, if you value your skin."

"Oh, indade, milady, indade."

Constance and Millicent looked at each other with the unspoken knowledge that the moment Lacey left the room, the gift of gloves would become common knowledge.

If Lacey had a penchant for gossip, she was also endowed with an uncanny ability to work wonders with silky fine hair. By the time she finished with Constance, Her Ladyship looked as if she had been coiffed by the Queen's own handmaiden.

The masses of blond hair had been swept up into a sleek twist that crowned the top of her head. A few ringlets were left to fall free and soften the somewhat severe style.

Jeremy commented upon her appearance as soon as he saw her. "You do me exceeding proud tonight, Lady Constance. I fear you will catch the Prince's eye and he will run off with you."

Constance gave him a dry look. "You have an undeniable talent for setting a lady down in such a charming way, sir."

He looked a trifle confused. "What did I say?"

She patted the folds of her skirt into place. "It was my understanding that the Regent was attracted only to women much older than he. Women such as Mrs. Fitzherbert."

Jeremy accepted the challenge with a twinkle in his eyes. "It was not my intention to set you down, as you well know. I only meant to say that the Prince has an eye for beauty." He drew his hand across his moustache as if stalling for time, then stood with his hands locked behind him. "And speaking of abilities, my lady, *you* have an undeniable ability for seeing criticism when none was intended. Can we not forgo our differences for one evening?"

Constance smiled sweetly and dropped a deep curtsey. "Your wish is but my command, my lord."

A hint of devilry lighted his slow smile. "Spoken like a true maiden. Now that you mention it, there is one small command," he said softly so that only she could hear.

She straightened abruptly and was ready to back away. "Don't you even dare to think such a thing. Now, do we stand here to gabble and clack or do we leave for Carlton House as you suggested?"

He laughed and the sound flooded the room with merriment. "Carlton House it is. May I assist you ladies with your cloaks?"

Millicent knotted her fan around her wrist. "Indeed you may. I am of course eager to see Carlton House, but what a pity the Regent will not likely be present."

Jeremy settled her cloak around her shoulders and turned to assist Constance. "Yes, 'tis a pity all right, but he is loath to be seen these days what with public opinion against him and the fact that he is so portly. Of course there is some chance he will make a brief appearance."

Constance stood still while Jeremy adjusted her cloak. She felt that he was taking an inordinately long time at it. Furthermore his hand chanced to press the back of her neck a little longer than was necessary or proper. She stole a look at Aunt Millicent, who appeared not to notice. Jeremy's face, however, bore an irritating look of pure innocence.

She turned to face him directly. "And speaking of the Prince, it was my impression that you were going to introduce me to him. Or was that just so much prattle?"

His eyes danced. "Lady Constance, you wound me. Surely you don't think I would deceive you."

"Don't I? I think you would do it with extreme pleasure."

"I'll admit I do take a certain pleasure in seeing you so agitated. It adds a blush of colour to your skin. Or perhaps it is only my company that brings such a rosy glow to your cheeks."

"If agitation is akin to irritation, that may well be true. Suffice it to say that we would be well advised to avoid one another tonight." The moment she said it she was sorry, for in truth, there was no one with whom she would rather spend her time.

Predictably, he outmaneuvered her by agreeing with her for a change. And so the prospects appeared grim that she would enjoy the endlessly long banquet that was reportedly so typical of an evening at Carlton House.

The ride to Carlton House in the carriage bearing the St. James crest was a quiet one until Jeremy reached across the space between them and picked up Constance's hand.

"I see you received my gift."

Constance was immediately contrite. "And I haven't even thanked you for them. You've kept me at such odds with myself that I am completely remiss in manners." She smiled sweetly. "The gloves are exquisite. Exactly what I would have chosen if I had seen them first. Forgive me for not mentioning them sooner, but we always seem to be at sword's point with one another and it chases everything else from my head."

The light from the carriage lantern cast brilliant highlights in her eyes, and Jeremy suddenly found it hard to breathe. He continued to hold her hand for an overlong time but Millicent chose not to reprimand him. Obligingly, she turned her head to feign interest in the parade of gaslights along Pall Mall.

"I kept the other glove long enough to know the correct size. My godmother said you searched for it." He stroked first one finger, then another, as he palmed her gloved hand between both of his. "I hope you were not overly embarrassed or put in an awkward position."

"Not at all," she lied. "I'm touched that you were concerned, but I'm even more moved by the thoughtfulness of your gift."

Jeremy was, for once, at a loss for words. In truth, his chest was tight with barely suppressed emotions. Although he felt he was making progress in his courtship of Lady Constance, it was so damnably easy to set her off. She was unusually independent for an unwed woman, but much of it annoyed and frustrated him, it was this very fact, along with her intelligence, wit and beauty, that attracted him to her.

At length she pulled her hand away, and he smiled and sat back against the plush cushions.

Constance regarded him through lowered lashes. For a moment there she thought he was going to say something more personal. There was a hooded expression in his eyes that made her heart beat faster. If they had been alone would he have spoken more freely? Or was it simply wishful thinking on her part?

He looked so elegant in his dove-grey trousers and matching waistcoat with darker grey piping. The frilled and ruffled shirt was of white silk and set off by a high starcher studded with a diamond stick pin. His doeskin gloves were also a soft dove grey.

The walk past the colonnaded entrance to Carlton House was not a short one, due to the number of carriages waiting to discharge passengers. The brick walkway was crowded by onlookers who were happy to have even a brief glimpse of the party goers. Constance was aware that the three of them made a handsome trio. Her heart stepped up its beat when she heard the music coming through the opened windows of the mansion.

How far she had come from her countrified life in Cornwall! And here she was in Carlton House—home of the Prince of Wales, the future King of England. But more important than that, she was with Jeremy St. James, Earl of Marshfield—and the most perfectly outrageous man she had ever met.

He squeezed her arm and looked down at her as if he knew exactly what she was thinking. The devil take him, she thought, for once hoping that he truly could read her mind.

They were no more inside the grand entrance than the three of them were swept up by acquaintances. Constance guessed that there must be well over a hundred people in attendance. They wandered from room to room, marvelling at the lavishly decorated walls, which were hung with silk and velvet paper and huge gilt mirrors in every conceivable place. They winked reflections of the elaborate gowns of silk, satin and velvet and the stunning array of jewels.

Millicent studied the porphyry columns, the magnificent chandeliers and the velvet carpets. ''I've never seen the like of it. It must indeed, for all its splendour, rival the Palace at Versailles.''

In the Golden Drawing Room, Lord Jeremy showed them the vista of the torchlighted gardens through broad windows, then moved on through the double doors of the library to another corridor. Just as they emerged, Constance heard an unwelcome voice and looked over her shoulder to see Lady Francine on her father's arm.

''Jeremy, darling!'' she exclaimed. ''I must apologize for being late. Father forgot to get my diamond necklace from the vault.''

Constance was too miffed to hear his reply. It took all her effort to keep a smile pasted on her face until Lady Francine and her father drifted off to join another group.

Constance felt Jeremy tense, and she immediately let go his arm. ''You didn't tell me that Lady Francine was to be among the guests tonight.''

''Should I have?''

She snapped her fan shut. ''Only if you wish to shield your name from the gossip mongers. But I perceive that you consider yourself above such gossip.''

''You perceive correctly. I have scant opportunity to listen to the flapping tongues of those who have little else to do with their time.''

Constance gave an unladylike snort. ''This can't be the same Lord Jeremy that *I* know. The one whose name is on the lips of every light-skirt in England. The one whose very name is synonymous with whoring and gaming.''

"That was the old Jeremy. I've done with gaming," he said mildly.

"And chasing after the demireps?" she added caustically.

His eyes narrowed. "Why would I chase demireps when I am in close pursuit of you, Lady Constance?"

She lifted her gaze to the heavens. "Spare me. I have no time for flattery."

"No flattery intended. But speaking of your time, what grand works and heroic deeds do *you* accomplish between the hours of dawn and dusk? Or do you spend your day sipping tea with fools such as Count Cianavelli, who I hear has set his sights on you?"

"Certainly not!" On the one hand she was secretly pleased that he appeared jealous, but on the other, she couldn't allow him to misunderstand. "Not that it is your concern, but Count Cianavelli is only a casual acquaintance. As for my time, I have a household to run as well as social engagements to consider."

"Hmm. It was my impression that the worthy Mr. and Mrs. Stavers saw to it that your house was kept in order."

"Yes, they are very capable."

"Leaving you free to seek your own pleasures?"

"I suppose that is quite true." A look of irritation flashed across her face. "Just what is it you are getting at, my lord?"

"Why, nothing. I was just trying to determine the difference between a man enjoying himself at the gaming table and a woman doing the same thing at her vanity table."

Constance set her chin at a sharp angle. "Stop trying to dilute the issue. There is no comparison, as you well know."

"I disagree. Times are changing. Many women can read and cipher nowadays. You yourself are well educated and able to speak articulately on many subjects, including the Corn Laws, as I'm told you demonstrated that night at Almack's."

Her mouth tightened. "Get to your point, my lord."

"My point is, Lady Constance, that you might look to improve yourself, instead of always levelling the finger at others."

She gave him a dry look. "Indeed. Perhaps I should put in my bid for a seat in Parliament."

He laughed. "You would get my support, but unfortunately, as a woman, you'd have to set your sights a bit lower."

Constance studied the planes of his face, the way his eyes regarded her with something akin to respect and admiration. Was it her imagination or was she seeing what she wanted to see? Still, what he said made good sense. For months now she had wanted to add a new dimension to her life, to work for some worthy cause. Aunt Millicent was already involved in a society to aid young chimney sweeps.

Still, Constance wasn't about to give Jeremy the satisfaction of being right. She opened her fan and waved it languidly in front of her face. "Someday, when I have my house in order, I may undertake some charitable pursuits. As for now, I have all I can do to keep up."

"Yes, I can see that." Jeremy noticed that Count Cianavelli was moving their way, his eye on Constance, and he touched her shoulder. "Beware of the Spanish one, my lady. He has an unsavory reputation for philandering."

Constance looked pointedly at Lord Jeremy. "That makes two of you." She turned to smile bewitchingly at Count Cianavelli. The Spaniard bowed low over her hand and kissed it. It was small wonder that the count had a reputation. He was a handsome man. Though of normal stature, his presence was striking, due mainly to a thatch of jet-black hair that waved away from his face and curled just below the tips of his ears. His eyes were dark and warm like melting drops of rich chocolate. And he liked women. Not just beautiful, rich women, but women of every age, status and physical description.

His deep, accented voice was like velvet as he said, "They tell me, Lady Constance, that the garden is exquisite. It would give me the greatest pleasure if you would consent to grace my arm for an exploration."

"Thank you, Count Cianavelli. I would be delighted." Turning to Jeremy, she said, "If you will excuse us, my lord? I'm sure Lady Francine must be longing for your company."

His eyes darkened and he bowed formally. "Then I shan't keep her waiting a moment longer."

Constance could have kicked herself. What purpose did it serve to fling him right into Lady Francine's arms—though he could have said he had better things to do. Was he trying to get back at Constance or had it been in his mind all along to go in search of his lady love?

Count Cianavelli held Constance's arm a little closer to him than she would have liked. When she made an attempt to move away, he only held her more tightly.

Constance firmly lifted his hand from her arm and looked over to where Aunt Millicent stood talking to the dowager duchess. "If we are to go into the garden, sir, I must inform my chaperon."

"My lady, do you not trust me?"

"Trust you? Don't be ridiculous. I was only thinking of the proprieties." She gave him a dry look. "I wouldn't want to ruin your reputation."

He threw his head back and laughed, at the same time attracting a good deal of attention. "My reputation would be ruined only if I could not seduce you, *mi belleza*."

If there was a single soul in the drawing room who hadn't heard him, Constance doubted it. Millicent looked up sharply, waiting for the signal from Constance to intervene. Though no one else could have noticed it, Constance arched her eyebrow and tilted her head toward Millicent and then toward the count.

The count stuck out his lower lip in a practised gesture. "Are you sure we haven't met somewhere in the past? I seem to remember your face. But no! How could one forget such a beautiful mouth?"

Constance forced a smile. "Surely you must know that if we had met, sir, I could hardly have forgotten you."

"That is true. It is possible, then, that I make a mistake."

"Be assured that you did." She turned. "Ah, here is my chaperon."

"Good evening again, Count Cianavelli," Millicent said. "If you will excuse us, Her Ladyship and I must freshen up before we dine."

He bowed. "*Ciertamente.* As you wish. I shall join you shortly. I have just been informed that we are to be dinner partners."

Constance would have questioned him, but he moved away before she had a chance. Moments later, Jeremy came toward her, his face contorted in anger.

"By all that is holy," he almost snarled, "you needn't have gone so far as to switch your place card. If my company is so unwelcome, all you have to do is say so."

Constance paled. "But, my lord..."

He didn't give her a chance to respond but turned and strode from the room. Millicent touched her fan to her chest. "Oh, my. Did you see his face? I fancy I've never seen him so outraged."

Constance had indeed seen his face. It was dusky red right down to his neckcloth. But it was his eyes that disturbed her. They were a bottomless blue, so dark that they appeared almost black. And this time there had been no hint of humour to soften their effect.

CHAPTER EIGHT

DINNER WAS AN EXPERIENCE. The guests were escorted to the table in the Gothic dining room in pairs, in the order of their importance. In the absence of the Regent, the Duke and Duchess of Heatherwood served as host and hostess. The meal began with green turtle soup, then the removes, or side dishes, and continued on to the serious business of main courses—great joints of beef and lamb, running with juices. They were followed by the sweets and savouries, ending, finally, with a dessert of fruit, nuts and bonbons.

Constance, sitting beside Count Cianavelli, had lost her appetite from the moment she chanced to look down the length of the table to see Lord Jeremy seated next to Lady Francine. After that, getting through the endless courses of food was almost unendurable. It was with considerable relief that Constance saw her hostess "collect eyes," which signalled the ladies that it was time to rise and leave the room. The gentlemen also rose.

As if on cue, Constance and Jeremy looked at each other. She wanted, more than anything, to go to him and explain that she had nothing to do with the placement of name cards, but the crush was too great. She was caught up in the exodus of women and was swept along to the drawing room.

Small talk was de rigueur, but when the women finally seated themselves in the drawing room, there was an indefinable tension, one that the duchess was unable to ease despite her considerable effort.

Lady Francine was laughing a little too loudly. Constance knew she was smiling a little too brightly. All the women seemed to be sitting on the edge of their chairs, until after some persuasion, Lady Francine arose and floated over to the pianoforte. After tastefully arranging her gown, she drifted a hand over the keys in a pretendedly random but harmonious passage. Then with both hands she played a liltingly suggestive piece that was pleasant to the ear, if rather long. There was genteel applause.

Miss Abernathy, one of Lady Francine's devotees, looked enraptured. "My dear lady, you honour Carlton House with your music. The Prince Regent will surely be disappointed to have missed this. You must tell us the name of that lovely piece. I don't believe I've heard it before."

Lady Francine bent her head to one shoulder in a charmingly demure gesture. "How sweet of you, Miss Abernathy. If truth be told, it is a little melody I wrote in fond remembrance of a romantic evening we spent in the Dark Walk at Vauxhall Garden."

The room was atwitter. Miss Abernathy fluttered her fan quickly as if overcome by the vapours. "We? Lady Francine, would that be you and a certain handsome rogue who just happens to live on an adjoining estate?"

Lady Francine raised her eyebrows in mock horror. "Merciful heaven. You can't ask me to kiss and tell, Miss Abernathy. At least not while my chaperon is nearby. She would never, absolutely never, permit me out of her sight again."

Before anyone could say anything she turned again to the pianoforte and began the chorus of "Secrets in the Dark," a popular, somewhat risqué song.

Millicent leaned toward Constance and whispered, "The bloody witch. She made up that little story about her romantic evening. I'll wager there's not a word of truth in it."

Constance was shocked, not so much by what Lady Francine had done but by her aunt's unheard-of use of vulgarity. She was about to say something when the duchess stood up.

"Is it my imagination or are the gentlemen lingering overlong at their port this evening?"

There was a general agreement that they were slow to return, and the duchess clasped her hands. "I wonder, Lady Constance, would it be an imposition to ask you to draw for us? We have heard of your remarkable talent."

Constance could scarcely refuse, though she was hardly in a mood now to be out in company, let alone draw sketches of simpering ladies. The duchess found some materials in a drawer and made a place for Constance under a glowing candelabrum.

After looking around, Constance decided to do a sketch of the room itself with just the vague impression of ladies seated in flowing gowns. More as a joke than anything, she sketched in the Prince Regent, in the military position of standing at ease. She had seen pictures of him when he was younger and less obese, and that was the way she drew him.

The entire sketch took less than twenty minutes. When it was finished, the ladies passed it around the room and exclaimed over it. By then the men were beginning to stroll into the drawing room.

Count Cianavelli carved a short path through the crowd to find a place immediately next to Constance. He smelled faintly of tobacco and port, not an unpleasant odour, unless compared to the clean, bayberry scent she was used to from Jeremy. She was tempted to move away but feared making a scene. Instead, she busied her hands with her fan.

The ivory handles were set with mother-of-pearl sticks, which held the vellum leaf. It was double-sided, one side bearing a painting of a castle set in the middle of a lake, the other depicting nymphs and satyrs cavorting in a leafy glade. It was a fan of some value, having been passed down from generation to generation for more than a hundred years.

Constance usually made it a point, while she fluttered her fan, to show the castle scene, because it was less gaudy, but tonight her thoughts were not on her fan. Absently she fluttered it in front of her face. The room was uncommonly warm. A curl on the left side of her head had begun to droop, and it tickled her ear. She brushed the fan against it as she listened halfheartedly to what the count was saying.

He stopped in midsentence, studied her for a brief instant, then continued with a degree of animation.

Constance looked around for Aunt Millicent, but she was involved in a conversation some few feet away.

Constance leaned forward to better hear what the count was saying. Again, the ringlet tickled her left ear and she brushed the curl aside with her open fan. Suddenly the room went quiet around her.

She wondered absently what was going on, but a surfeit of food and the longing to go home had made her too drowsy to care.

The count leaned closer and spoke in a low, seductive voice. "Whatever it is, *señorita,* you have my word." He moistened his upper lip. "*Bella mia,* the dancing will begin soon in the ballroom. Would you favor me with a waltz if there is room on your card?"

"I . . . yes. If not a waltz, a mazurka, perhaps."

He made a face. "*Por favor.* The waltz is so much more romantic."

"Precisely the problem."

He pretended to be hurt, but there was a smile at the corners of his eyes. "They were right when they said you are very independent and somewhat of an adventuress?"

"I beg your pardon?"

He smiled. "It was a compliment, my lady, but I see your friend approaching and he appears rather irate." The count swept a grand bow. "Perhaps it is wise if I leave now. Until later?"

Constance nodded just as Lord Jeremy, without so much as a by-your-leave, took her by the arm and directed her to follow him.

"What do you think you are doing?" she demanded.

"I'm going to show you the conservatory. What did you think I was going to do?"

"Murder and mayhem crossed my mind, from the unseemly way you're dragging me out of here. Do let go of my arm."

Millicent followed them to the door. "Is everything all right, my dear?"

Jeremy inclined his head and answered for Constance. "Everything is fine, or will be in a few minutes. May I beg to speak to Lady Constance alone?"

Millicent frowned. "Well, I—"

"We'll be in the conservatory, Aunt Millicent. I doubt that we will be entirely alone."

"Very well, if you insist. But I shan't be far away."

Jeremy eased the pressure on Constance's arm, but the set of his face did little to hide his determination to speak to her.

"Did it not occur to you, Lady Constance, that you are courting trouble when you play up to a man like Count Cianavelli?"

"What do you mean, play up to him? I've only met the man a few times."

"I find that hard to believe. You're making a laughingstock of yourself. Thanks to the duchess, I got to you in time."

"In time for what?"

He swore competently. "The business of the fan. Did you think no one could see it?"

"It's only a picture, my lord. And quite a famous one at that. *Nymphs and Satyrs in Echo Wood* by Grimaldi. It belonged to my grandmother."

"Are you playing me for the fool?"

She was fast losing patience. "If I were, my lord, you would not have to ask me. Look," she said, half opening the fan and touching it to her lips. "The fan is old but the painting is far from indecent. In fact, it is often admired by people who recognize quality."

He groaned and turned away from her to rest his hands and then his head on a bronze statue of a stag. "I believe I have aged a lifetime since I was fortunate enough to rescue you from a certain death."

"If you had not been visiting a house of ill repute you would have nothing to complain about. In truth, we may have both been better off."

"You think you would be better off dead?" Surprise and something akin to pain edged his voice.

"Of course not." She lifted her eyes to him. "I simply meant that I would have recovered on my own."

"That is highly unlikely."

She raised her shoulder and made a gesture with her fan to show her complete disdain.

He grabbed her hand and held it gently but immobile. "Will you put that damnable fan away before I break your arm?"

Appalled, Constance pulled away. "How dare you speak to me in such a way!"

"You asked for it, you know—flirting with me that way, the same way that you've been flirting with the count ever since we arrived."

Constance looked around her. "Am I daft or is this some kind of nightmare? Whatever are you talking about, my lord? I flirted with no one. Least of all with

Count Cianavelli." She closed her fan and absently drew it across her cheek.

His eyes grew thoughtful. "Is it possible that you don't know?" He shook his head. "No. I find that far too convenient."

"Know what, Jeremy?" she demanded, then realized too late that she had forgotten to use his title.

But apparently he didn't notice because he reached over and carefully slipped the fan from her wrist.

"Lady Constance, in the past ten minutes you have told the count that you always long to be near him. That you want him to keep your secret. You've told me to wait for you, that I may kiss you, that you always long to be near me, and you've asked me if I love you."

"What!" she demanded. "I did no such thing." Her voice had begun to sound as if it belonged to a fishwife, but she was powerless to control it.

He shook his head in disbelief. "Then it's true. You do not understand the language of the fan?"

"I...no." She touched her fingers to her cheek. "I...I do seem to remember some casual mention of it, that messages could be passed from one to another by means of a fan. But when I was a debutante my father thought it more important that I learn languages, and to cipher, and..." She felt the heat begin to crawl into her face. "Great lackaday! I had no idea. No wonder everyone was staring at me."

Jeremy suddenly felt as if a wagonload of oats had been lifted from his shoulders. He began to chuckle softly, then threw his head back and laughed. "One way or another, Constance, you are bound to be in the public eye, it seems. I would advise you to be careful how you display your fan. There are those who take the messages very seriously.''

She let out her breath. "And do you, my lord?" she asked. He studied the question in her eyes, the honey-blond lashes as they swept downward, the soft curve of her mouth, tremulous now as she waited.

He cleared his throat, but his voice was still husky when he spoke. "My Lady Constance. Had I believed for a moment that you meant what you were saying when you flashed your fan in my direction, you would surely not be standing here now in all your jewels and finery. For I would take you to bed so quickly that time itself would lose all meaning."

Constance drew a deep, shuddering breath. She should have chastised him. She should have stopped him from saying such outrageous things. But instead, she stood there looking at him, her mouth slightly agape, her hand paused midway between her bosom and her mouth.

Jeremy was entranced. It was all he could do to keep from taking her in his arms and carrying her off to his carriage. But common sense took over, and he reached for her hands.

"Here. Take your wayward fan. In the future, my lady, be careful what you do with it."

He held her hands overlong, but she made no effort to pull away. Jeremy felt a surge of desire so strong that it threatened to smother him. Another time, in such a mood, he might have driven his team hell-bent to The Tart Shoppe, but Arabella's girls no longer appealed to him.

He released Constance out of self-preservation and stepped back a pace, his hands locked behind him to keep them from shaking.

"May I beg the honour of the first dance, Lady Constance?"

She curtsied. "The honour is mine, sir." He offered his arm and she placed her gloved hand on it. The fan was securely folded and placed in the safety of a velvet pannier.

As was customary, the first dance after dinner was a lively French quadrille with groups of four couples participating in the five-figured dance. The music began and the dancers moved to the centre, hands linked. It was difficult for Constance to concentrate on the intricacies of the dance when Jeremy was holding her hand so firmly in his own. Even through the fabric of her gloves she was aware of the messages being sent and received, as if her senses intermingled with his of their own volition.

The Fagans, a couple directly across from Constance and Jeremy, were newly married. Constance found Mrs. Fagan to be both friendly and intelligent. Her cap of red hair and snubbed nose, which was dusted with freckles, made her look even younger than her nineteen years.

When the sets ended, Mrs. Fagan asked Constance to join her in a foray to the guest chamber to freshen themselves. Constance was only too willing, for the room was overheated, and she had to resist several times the urge to use her fan to cool herself. After telling Millicent, who was deep in conversation with a young officer of the Guard, where she was going,

Constance set off with Mrs. Fagan, who lifted the corner of her bright yellow satin skirt and led the way. "I mustn't be overlong. My husband becomes completely unsettled when I'm out of his sight." She said it with a touch of pride that was sure indication of her newlywed state.

"He's an unusually handsome man, Mrs. Fagan."

"Thank you, but no more handsome than Lord Jeremy. Do please call me Sarah. I sometimes forget to answer when someone calls me Mrs. Fagan."

"Then you must call me Constance."

"Oh? Are you sure it's proper? I mean, you *are* highborn."

"Of course it's proper. Besides, I'm from the country, Cornwall to be exact. Our ways are more relaxed than they are here in London."

"Yes, I know. I've heard of you and have been wanting to meet you."

"Indeed?" Constance wasn't sure she wanted to hear more, but the earnest young woman went on.

"Talk of your concern for the plight of the farmers has reached us, and I have been trying to summon courage to ask you to join our little group, who have been protesting the enforcement of the Corn Laws." She said it all of a breath and when she was done she was breathing hard. When Constance didn't answer immediately, the woman appeared somewhat embarrassed.

"I beg your forgiveness if I have overstepped myself, Your Ladyship, but the need is so great that I had to risk your displeasure."

"No, you have no reason to fear on that score. I was merely trying to think of what possible help I could be. It is true I do support the movement to repeal the Corn Laws, but there is little hope that Parliament will do anything about it. You see, most of the large holdings belong to members of Parliament who are gentlemen farmers."

"I know. And they are unlikely to pass laws that will help the small landowners and hurt themselves."

"Precisely."

Sarah's face sobered. "Of course. I understand, and I do not bear you any ill because you refused to join us."

"Oh, but I didn't refuse," Constance assured her. "If truth be told, I have been thinking seriously about spending more time to help those who are deprived. If you will advise me of your next meeting, I shall endeavour to accompany you, at least to enquire into the organization."

They talked a little more as they fussed with their hair and checked their skirts in the ladies' room. The more they talked, the more Constance liked the young woman. Compared to the shallow, twittering young ladies who were in current vogue, Sarah Fagan seemed to have a remarkable depth of character and a genuine sense of purpose. Was it marriage and the responsibilities that went with the state that made the youthful couple appear so intelligent and mature?

Of late Constance had found something lacking in her own life. Once the work of refurbishing her house had been finished, she had noticed a certain void. When she mentioned it to Millicent, her aunt had laughingly said that it was nothing that couldn't be cured by the right man. But Constance wasn't so sure that was the solution. Perhaps Lord Jeremy had been right when he said she needed another direction for her energies.

The women returned to the ballroom to find Oliver Fagan standing with Jeremy, both listening to Lady Francine and apparently oblivious to everything else in the room.

Lady Francine shook her shoulders slightly so that her dress shimmered bewitchingly around her slim figure, then put her hand to her cheek in a coy gesture. "So I said to the duke, 'Why, you terrible man. If Daddy heard you say such a deplorable thing he would have you transported to the hinterlands.'"

The two men laughed, hardly taking their eyes from her face. Constance set her chin. "That woman is beginning to get under my skin."

Sarah considered the situation with a knowing frown. "She has her cap set on Lord Jeremy. I hope it is your intention to fight for him. She is nothing more than a spoiled child."

Constance sighed. "I fear I have no claim on him, but I confess I do have a certain yearning." Constance was surprised at her confession. She had not been so frank even with Aunt Millicent.

Sarah wrinkled her freckled nose. "Then why are we standing here and allowing her to run off with the horse and carriage?"

"Why indeed?" Constance said as they moved forward to join the group.

The men moved aside to make room for them in the small circle. Lady Francine edged closer to Jeremy and tucked her arm in his. Oliver Fagan circled his arm around his wife's waist in such an unconscious gesture of endearment that Constance felt a lump in her throat. How wonderful it must be to be loved so completely and to love so completely in return.

She was hardly aware of the conversation until Lady Francine lifted her hand to her ear in a delicate gesture. "Listen. Is that not a waltz? Jeremy, dear, you promised to dance with me again."

Jeremy looked toward Constance and reached up to adjust his cravat. Sarah Fagan was quick to seize the moment.

"Lady Francine, there is something my husband and I would love to show you. It's in the collection of paintings the Regent has on display downstairs. You must see it. One of the ladies is so lovely...the very picture of you. I wondered if there might be some family connection?"

Lady Francine was visibly flattered, so much so that she failed to notice the bewildered expression on Mr. Fagan's face.

Sarah Fagan gave her husband a look and took his arm. "Come, darling. Let's take Lady Francine downstairs and show her the painting we talked about."

Before either of them had a chance to protest, Sarah Fagan was steering them in the direction of the grand staircase.

Constance met Jeremy's gaze and their eyes locked. He didn't speak. His look said everything as he held out his arms and she went into them.

There were those, Lord Byron in particular, who said that the newfangled waltz was just an excuse to touch and feel the opposite sex. Constance wasn't put off. Fact of the matter was, she was looking forward to it.

CHAPTER NINE

THE MUSIC BEGAN to swell, and on the dance floor couples whirled and floated to the romantic strains of "The Isolde Waltz." Jeremy was finding it ridiculously hard to breathe. His hand, placed sedately in the centre of Lady Constance's back, held her at a proper distance, but he couldn't stop wondering how it would be to hold her close in his arms, the length of her pressed against him....

Even at arm's distance the scent of her perfume intoxicated his senses until he wanted to snatch the pins from her hair and bury his face in it.

He cupped his fingers around her hand and stroked the top of it, sensing rather than feeling her intake of breath. There was the briefest hesitation, and then her fingers curled around his hand in an answering caress. Her eyes darkened with an awareness that sent a shaft of desire shooting through him and he pulled her closer. She offered no resistance. For the first time in his adult life Jeremy was moved by an emotion so strong that it surpassed anything he had ever experienced.

In as close an embrace as decorum allowed, they danced a single turn around the floor. Constance loved the shelter of his arms, loved the way his thigh brushed hers as they whirled and dipped in the intricate patterns of the waltz, loved the way they moved as a single entity.

But when they approached the alcove where Aunt Millicent was seated, the older women caught Jeremy's eye and shook her head. Constance, too, saw the slight gesture and could gladly have struck her aunt dead for choosing that precise moment to enact her role of chaperon. With a sigh, Jeremy moved back enough to separate them to a more modest degree. Again they were at arm's length and Constance felt as if she had lost a part of herself.

All too soon the music ended. Instead of leaving the floor, Jeremy stood there, refusing to release her hand, though surely he must have been aware that they were being watched by more than a dozen pairs of eyes. Constance, still smarting over the fiasco of the fan, made a move to step away, but he shook his head.

"No. Stay."

Count Cianavelli came up from behind Jeremy and touched his shoulder. "*Señor,* I believe the next dance is mine."

The earl's voice was low, but his tone was unmistakable. "Then your belief is incorrect, sir. The next dance is mine."

Count Cianavelli, his olive skin turning darker still, looked pointedly at Constance.

"My lady?"

Constance was at a loss. She knew that two successive dances with the same man was considered improper behaviour for an unmarried woman and could compromise her reputation. Moreover, she had indeed promised the dance to the count. She looked at the count, then at Jeremy, whose expression was infinitely compelling.

"Forgive me, Count Cianavelli," she said, without taking her eyes away from Jeremy's bottomless gaze. And then the music began, and once again they were caught up in the all-encompassing magic.

It was as if time were suspended. In his arms Constance felt a surrender of will that was foreign to her until this moment. She floated, hardly aware that her feet touched the ground. As if guided by some inner compass they moved effortlessly between the other dancers, yet never once did his gaze leave her face.

Three minutes was an eternity, yet the time vanished in the blink of an eye as once again the music ceased. With an obvious effort, Jeremy released her and stepped back with a practised bow. She curtsied and a smile curved her mouth.

Immediately they were approached by a uniformed man wearing large gold epaulets. He reminded Constance that his name was next on her card. She looked at Jeremy, started to speak and then was at a loss for words.

Jeremy took her arm. "Her ladyship requires a breath of air, admiral. I know you will excuse her," he said, steering her toward the door.

"But I would gladly escort her to the terrace if she—"

He didn't have a chance. Jeremy ignored him as if he didn't exist. Taking Constance by the hand, he cut his way though the crowd with the authority and determination of a leader confronting his troops.

Constance looked back with chagrin over her shoulder toward the disappointed admiral. She must take pains later to make amends for her unseemly behavior. Ignoring his name on the dance card was worse than improper. It implied that she and Jeremy were betrothed, or at the very least, that they were having an affair. When she turned again to reprimand Jeremy she suddenly forgot the proprieties and focused her entire being on Jeremy and her need for him. The fact that he apparently felt the same need was too incredible for her to put a name to it.

At length they reached the comparative privacy of the terrace with its wide stone floor set with trees in marble tubs that punctuated the outside wall. A few couples had also taken the opportunity to speak privately, but Constance and Jeremy were separated by distance and the blessing of semidarkness. Torches cast flickering shadows over the stone work and along the walk that led to a darkened labyrinthian garden. Jeremy would have chosen that path but Constance held back.

"No, Jeremy. You know we can't flout convention to such an extreme."

"Why not? Isn't it a question of courage?"

"No. I think not."

"Then what, pray tell? Surely you have no one to answer to but yourself and, of course, your aunt."

"There you have it, I think, not to mention the fact that we are guests of the Regent and it would be less than prudent to break the rules, even if they are unwritten."

"Isn't it time we make our own rules?"

A smile curved the corners of her mouth. "Now you sound like a little boy who can't have his own way."

He laughed. "I suppose there is truth to what you say but I detest such foolishness." His voice was husky. "Especially now."

"Indeed? Why now in particular?"

He saw the intensity, the warmth deep in her eyes, and he reached for her hands. "Need you ask, Constance? We both know that something is happening to us. Something that began the moment I lifted you in my arms that night at The Tart Shoppe. I felt it then, I feel it whenever I'm with you, but tonight the feeling is so strong that it defies reason."

She stood there for a breathless moment waiting to hear more, waiting for the words that would bind her to him forever. But she waited in vain.

Slowly she pulled her hands away and held them tightly together beneath the folds of her shawl.

She sighed. "I'll grant you, my lord, that there is some truth to what you say. There is a certain eloquence to the music coming from the ballroom that makes one forget all else but the present. But what happens when tomorrow dawns? Will we return to sword's point?"

He turned abruptly and leaned his elbows on the stone balustrade. "Egad, woman. You have a knack for cutting me down."

"Such was not my intention. We are friends, perhaps even a bit more than friends. In truth, I freely admit that I am drawn to you by some strange force that I am loath to name."

"Love, damn it. Why should you be afraid to say it?"

She laughed sharply and without humour. "You ask *me*? If you think on it, sir, this is the first time the word 'love' has left your mouth—at least in *my* presence. Suffice it to say that with other women you have doubtless used the word as often as you salted your potatoes."

He swore softly. "Love has never entered the picture until now."

"Lady Francine would be the first to argue the point."

He shot a dark look at her. "Don't forget my French teacher. I wanted to marry her when I was twelve. Will you also throw that up to me?"

"The situation is hardly the same."

He sighed and wiped his hand across his face. "Francine is almost like a sister. We grew up together, and yes, there was a time once when I returned from boarding school and saw her all grown up, that I thought we might marry, but that is long since forgotten. I care for her as a friend, nothing more." There was a long silence during which they both appeared to search their feelings.

"Constance, don't let us debate each other. I care for you more than I've cared for any woman in my life."

"And I care for you—perhaps a good deal more than I should."

She saw that he gripped the balustrade with all his strength, then slowly relaxed. His voice was low and husky when he spoke.

"Then that is a beginning. Would it be asking too much of you to refuse to be courted by other men until we can determine just how deep our feelings run?"

Constance was ready to throw her arms around him and swear her allegiance for eternity, but at that moment a page in crimson livery approached them and snapped to attention as he presented Sir Jeremy with a message on a silver plate.

He scanned it quickly, then read it again before he addressed the page. "Go at once and say that I will be there in a moment." When the boy scampered away, Jeremy turned back to Constance, his brow furrowed.

"I am deeply sorry, Constance. I have to go."

"Indeed? Is something wrong? Is there anything I can do?"

"No. I have no time to explain. My only regret is that I must leave you at such a time." He ran his fingers through his hair. "The errand should take only a short while. I'll be back to see you and your aunt safely home."

"I understand."

He took her arm and escorted her inside to where Aunt Millicent was waiting. Then with little more than a perfunctory bow, he excused himself.

Millicent raised her eyebrow. "Was it something I said, or was it perhaps because I chastised him for his unseemly behaviour on the dance floor?"

"No, though I personally could have strangled you. You had nothing to do with his departure now. Jeremy received an urgent message and had to leave."

"How untoward. Did he say whom the message was from?"

"I didn't ask. He assured me, however, that he would return in time to escort us home."

Millicent looked pleased. "I'll venture to say that he is becoming more than a token friend." She tapped Constance's arm with the tip of her finger. "But watch yourself, my girl, or you will create a scandal. Half the tongues in the room were wagging over the way he danced the waltz with you. And two dances in a row. Indeed!"

"The scandal-mongers will always find something to talk about."

"That is true, but you risk your chances with Lord Jeremy if you court scandal so openly. I'm told that his mother is something of an ogre when it comes to keeping a good name."

"She should have thought of it when she was raising her son. His name is at the top of every gossip's list."

"Tut-tut, Constance. Don't behave like a child. You know the rules are different for men."

Constance was about to demand to know why it should be that way when they were approached by Lady Sefton. They chatted for a few minutes, then Lady Sefton walked with them to view the paintings on display in one of the corridors.

Lady Sefton, looking matronly and kind and yet elegant in a buttery yellow taffeta gown set off with a stunning diamond-and-sapphire necklace, tucked her hands in her sleeves.

"I'm so sorry Lord Jeremy had to leave so abruptly, Lady Constance. If you and Miss Seaforth should chance to need a ride back to The Beeches, our carriage is large and you are most welcome to join us."

"Thank you, Lady Sefton. You are most kind. However, Lord Jeremy expects to return shortly."

"In truth? From the expression on Lady Francine's face when they left together, I surmised that he would not be returning tonight."

Constance felt her face freeze. So he had left with Lady Francine. The devil take him!

Millicent, who was quick to recognize how Constance was feeling, smiled warmly. "You are more than generous, Lady Sefton, but we do have other arrangements."

"Very well, perhaps another time. We must have tea one day soon. The two of you have brought such delightful new life to London society since you arrived here. We count ourselves privileged to have you among us."

She didn't wait for a response but merely nodded and swept off to join a group of women on the other side of the room.

"New life, indeed." Millicent sniffed. "What she meant was new fodder for the gossip mills."

"Don't be too quick to judge, Aunt Millicent. I'm sure she meant to be kind. Besides—" Constance regarded her aunt dryly "—you said it yourself, Aunt Millicent. It's better to be talked about than ignored."

"Well...if I said it, I suppose it's true."

Constance laughed, despite her growing depression. Jeremy was near to losing a staunch supporter in Aunt Millicent when he so quickly departed with Lady Francine on his arm. Nevertheless, her aunt would be the last to admit she had misjudged someone.

The rest of the evening seemed an eternity. Carlton House with its gilt and glitter had lost its attractions when Jeremy left with Lady Francine. Even the remote hope that the Prince Regent would make a late appearance held little appeal for Constance. Many of the guests had left nearly an hour ago. She, too, wanted to go home.

Millicent darted a quick look at Constance. "Pinch your cheeks, child. You look peaky."

"I feel peaked." She swung around irritably and caught her skirt on a marble pedestal. "Toadflax! Jeremy has put us in a devilish position. If we send for a hack it will look as if we've been left at the altar, so to speak." She gave her skirt a yank. "Is there a soul here, I wonder, who is disabused of the fact that Jeremy left with Lady Francine?"

"He could have had a good reason," Millicent observed doubtfully.

"Neither of us believes that, nor does anyone else. Come. I'm tired of waiting for him. I'm going to beg a ride from a new friend."

"A discreet one, I hope."

"I wager we'll find out in a few days." Constance couldn't hide the disappointment in her voice.

Mr. and Mrs. Oliver Fagan were most gracious when Constance asked them if they would drive Millicent and her to The Beeches. When they arrived,

Constance invited them to come in, but they declined.

Constance collected her shawl around her. "I can't thank you enough for your kindness. I'm looking forward to seeing you at the next meeting of the reform group."

Oliver Fagan cradled his top hat between his hands. "We are having a small gathering at our home in ten days. If you would care to join us, my wife will see to it that you are sent an invitation."

"Please do. It is time I learned more about the plight of our farmers."

Oliver saw the women to the door and took his leave.

Once inside, Aunt Millicent looked askance as they went upstairs.

"Are you sure you're doing the right thing, getting involved with radicals?"

"They are hardly radicals, Aunt Millicent. They are merely concerned citizens. Regardless, I need something to do. We were always kept busy seeing after our people in Cornwall." She stopped at the door to her bedchamber and faced her aunt. "Here I feel as if I spend most of my time changing costumes, getting ready to go out, or just having returned, or waiting on guests."

"But that's what the London Season is. If one isn't sought after, one is considered a failure. You're tired, Constance, and overset because Lord Jeremy behaved in such a cavalier fashion. Tomorrow will cast a different light on it."

THE SUN HAD NOT BEEN UP long when Mr. Stavers sent Lacey to awaken her mistress. Lacey carried a pot of hot cocoa to soften the blow.

Constance squinted her eyes and groaned. "I trust that what you have to say is worth risking your life."

Lacey grinned. "Indade, Your Ladyship. 'Tis 'imself who is 'ere. Lord Jeremy 'as shown 'is card and wishes to speak wi' you."

Constance dropped back down on the bed. "He does, does he? Well, you may tell my lord Jeremy St. James that I have no wish to see him. Now or ever."

Lacey dropped her mouth open. "But I thought you 'n' 'im were close to postin' the banns."

Constance sat up again, snatched the card from the salver and tore it in half. "There's that for Lord Jeremy and you have my permission to tell him so. Now be so good as to leave me alone."

Lacey had sense enough to depart and close the door after her while she was still in one piece.

Constance drew her knees up to her chin. Suddenly her life seemed to stretch out endlessly before her. The London parties and routs that had seemed so appealing back in Cornwall now were just so much clack and gabble, something to get through. Unaccountably, she felt an emptiness that ached to be filled; a longing to be needed, to be a necessary part of someone's life.

It took considerable effort to force herself to get out of bed. She threw on a wrapper and went to close the window. Chancing to look down to the courtyard below, she saw Jeremy's carriage waiting in the drive. He was standing next to it, looking at the house as if uncertain what to do next.

"The devil take him!" she said, then drew the draperies hard across the view.

Anyone living at The Beeches during the next few days could easily have given an account of what it was like to live inside a tropical storm. Lady Constance drove the staff to its limit—cleaning, scraping, polishing every inch of the house until it smelled of lemon oil and beeswax and lavender from the attic to the darkest cellar. She drove herself equally hard.

Each day Stavers delivered a card from Sir Jeremy, asking permission to see her. Each day she held the card for a moment, then wordlessly shook her head and replaced it on the salver.

She could overlook the fact that Jeremy had left her alone at the mercy of the gossips, but for him to leave with Lady Francine was more than Constance could bear. It reminded her too much of her father's cavalier behavior toward the women in his life.

On Thursday, their at-home day, Constance shut herself in her room and refused to see anyone. She knew that Millicent was holding court in the salon and making excuses for the absence of her niece, but Constance cared little one way or the other.

By the second Thursday Millicent had lost her patience and good humour. She drew herself up to her full five feet two inches and propped her hands on her hips. "I've had enough of this, my girl. I'm through making excuses for you. It's time you stopped playing the recluse and started seeing people."

Constance studied her with quiet regard. "I know you think it's for the best, Aunt Millicent, but I truly am not ready to see anyone. In a few days we will be

going to the country to visit the Fagans. Until then..."
She shrugged, leaving the sentence unfinished.

Constance knew that she had not been so completely withdrawn since the death of her mother. Although she knew it was a temporary indisposition, there was nothing she could do to stave off the dark oppression. Her sketchbook, which at one time seemed to hold an infinite number of empty sheets, was being filled at an amazing rate. In truth, thumbing through the pages as she sat in the gazebo at the back of the garden, Constance was appalled at the amount of time she had spent with little more than pencil and pad to occupy her.

She was shading in the stonework on a drawing of the lion's-head fountain set in the mossy wall behind the gazebo when a shadow crossed the page. Looking up, she saw Jeremy, hat in hand, observing her. He swept a low bow.

"Lady Constance."

"Indeed. At least you have the right name. How difficult it must be to keep your women disentangled." She snapped the sketchbook shut. "What are you doing here? I've made it clear I don't wish to see you."

"I don't understand your change of heart. Suffice it to say that you have a right to be overset because I left Carlton House so abruptly the eve of the Regent's party."

"Overset is putting it far too mildly. I have every right to be furious, my lord, and I wager you would be wise not to put my mood to the test."

"So I gather. On the other hand, Constance, do I not deserve an opportunity to explain?"

She reached down for her bonnet, which lay on the stone bench. Jeremy's chest tightened uncomfortably when she bent her head and the sunlight picked up highlights of gold and bronze and pale yellow in her unbound hair. She answered him without looking up.

"It is unnecessary to explain anything to me," she said. "I understood perfectly."

He appeared truly puzzled. "I can't understand why you are so angry. I left a message and made other arrangements for you to be taken home. If I could have returned I would have, but I couldn't leave my mother."

Constance lifted her eyes. "My lord, don't make it worse than it already is. I received no message. Let's do put an end to it now, before . . ." She couldn't trust her voice to finish.

He saw the pain in her eyes and knew full well he was the cause of it. Once again he wished he had lived his life more honourably. He would have given anything for her to trust him.

She had collected her things and risen. "You must excuse me. I beg of you, my lord. Don't come here again. I think it best if . . . if in the future, we don't see one another."

His voice shook. "You can't mean that, Constance."

"But I do."

He reached for her arm and held it so that she couldn't leave. "Why are you doing this to us when you know that we are meant to be together?"

She saw the anguish in his eyes and wondered how he could sound so genuine and yet behave so badly.

"Let me go, Jeremy," she whispered.

"Then say that you will hear me out."

A part of her cried out to feel his arms around her, but another part remembered the triumph written on Lady Francine's face. She shook her arm free and walked away. Jeremy did not follow.

CHAPTER TEN

IN A TIME when no gentleman boasted of working and no lady would ever be caught doing what could be done for her, Oliver and Sarah Fagan were the exception. It occurred to Constance that this was the very reason she liked them. There was a basic goodness in the way they spoke to their servants and the consideration they gave the tenant farmers who worked their lands.

The small band of radicals, as Millicent insisted on calling them, had met for nearly four hours in an effort to map out ways to ease the ever-worsening predicament of the farmers. The postwar slumps were always the most oppressive. Now that the unfortunate war with the United States had ended in New Orleans, the future boded ill for the small landholder. The price of wheat, considered the bellwether of the economy, had risen to one hundred twenty-six shillings a bale; a boon for the landed gentry but a death knell for the poor classes.

Some fifteen concerned citizens had gathered in the Fagans' drawing room. To Constance, they were strangers, all. When she saw how eagerly they leaned into the task of righting the wrongs brought about by Parliament's unwise decisions, she sympathized with them and puzzled over how she might contribute her share.

Since her arrival in London she had made a passing acquaintance with Morton Gadsworth, associate editor of the London Daily *Times*. Because of her connections, the group decided her efforts would lie in the direction of putting the farmer's plight before the public eye.

She was making a list of the people who she thought might hold a degree of influence when the butler entered the room and spoke softly to Mrs. Fagan. The news brought a quick smile.

"Yes, of course. Do send him in at once."

The room grew silent. Sarah folded her hands and addressed the group. "It seems we have a guest. Although I know some of you will resent his presence because of what he represents, I give you my word that he is a man of honour and will be an asset to our cause."

At that moment Jeremy St. James entered the room as the butler announced him. There were sudden murmurs of protest, which were silenced by the Fagans. Lord Jeremy stood, his hands locked behind him, his expression grave as he spoke.

Constance was so aware of his physical presence that she could not have repeated a single word he said during the next five minutes. She feasted her gaze on him, knowing that she should make every effort to avoid him, yet savouring the moment for as long as possible. Had he followed her here, or was it mere chance that had brought him to the country? She pulled her glance away from Jeremy and saw the smile of satisfaction on her hostess's face. Apparently fate had been given a hand in the guise of Sarah Fagan.

What he said must have reassured those assembled because they made room for him in their midst. Millicent appeared more than pleased to see him—and not entirely surprised. Was everyone conspiring against her? Constance wondered.

She tried to concentrate on the subject at hand, but she was too unsettled to hear more than on occasional word. It was as if the room and its occupants had become a stage and she was off in the wings, more observer than participant. She wrapped her arms around herself in an unconscious gesture of self-preservation. She experienced an overwhelming feeling of being swept away on a fast-moving tide.

The meeting lasted another hour, or was it two? Constance lost all track of time and place as she mentally withdrew. Only the two of them existed. Jeremy, looking drained and far from his usual devil-may-care self, lost council of his eyes more than once as their gaze met and held. Constance wanted to look away but found it impossible.

Neither managed a smile. Their hurt had gone too deep to be so easily healed.

Jeremy gripped the edges of his chair. By all that was holy, he would not let another day go by until he made his peace with Constance. He would make her understand that she meant everything to him. And then as surely as if a veil had suddenly lifted, he knew beyond any possible doubt that he wanted to take her to wife. The realization came with a blinding force that staggered him. It was as if he had suddenly discovered the meaning of the word destiny.

He looked at Constance and smiled.

The light in his eyes and the warmth of his smile startled her. She looked away and refused to meet his gaze again.

The meeting dragged on, but still Constance didn't hear a word. When it was over everyone gathered more closely and she managed to work her way to the outside of the group in order to execute a quick departure. But it wasn't to be. Jeremy, who had been speaking to Aunt Millicent, elbowed his way through the guests and caught up with her.

"I've sent your driver on home so that—"

"You what!" she demanded. "You have a nerve."

"Apparently that is what it takes, my lady. I've been trying to see you for days, but you have made it impossible."

"And with good reason, sir. A gentleman would take the hint and accept it with grace."

"You've never counted me a gentleman. As I recall, you've called me a rakehell and a rogue but never a gentleman."

"Your actions speak well for my judgement."

Jeremy noticed that they were attracting attention. "Perhaps we should take our leave. We have an errand first, and then my coach is at your disposal."

Constance sighed. "I suppose I have little choice in the matter, but if it is your intention to leave my chaperon behind, you had better think again, sir."

He permitted himself a smile. "I wouldn't dream of it. Your aunt is waiting for us to give her the nod."

"I shan't forgive you for this, Jeremy."

"A fact that I already regret, Constance. It is my hope that given time, I might be able to change your opinion of me."

He was far too quick for her. That fact surprised her, for she had always held her own in any verbal sparring match. But instinct told her that silence was the one weapon he was powerless to fight.

While Sir Jeremy rousted the driver, Constance paid her respects to Sarah and Oliver and said goodbye to the other guests.

Sarah looked distraught. "I do hope I did the right thing. It was I who told Lord Jeremy that you would be here today."

Constance patted Sarah's hand. "No harm done," she said, and hoped it sounded convincing, "but I must admit I was surprised to see him. Is he one of your regulars?"

Oliver Fagan raked his fingers through his thatch of sandy hair. "Lord Jeremy is a sympathizer, though not a bona-fide member of our group. He has aided us, though had never met with us until today."

Sarah smiled bewitchingly. "You ought to have seen him the day he visited Oliver and me. We made the rounds of some of the smaller farms. Lord Jeremy was as good as one of them, holding a pitchfork and all got up in his fustians and a big straw hat." They laughed together at the picture Sarah created. Then Jeremy returned to say that the carriage was waiting at the porte-cochère.

They had driven a good three miles before Constance chanced to looked out the curtained window.

She realized they were going the wrong direction and straightened abruptly.

"Of all the . . . Where are you taking us, sir?"

"I told you we had an errand to perform before I take you home."

"You failed to mention that it would seriously delay our return."

He grinned. "Did I indeed? Yes, by jove, I think you are right. But no. I think I informed your aunt. Is that not true?" he asked, looking at Millicent with raised eyebrows.

"Quite true." Her expression was halfway between a smile and a frown, a sure sign that something was amiss.

Constance studied her aunt's face. Yes, something was definitely going on here. The two of them were in a conspiracy against her. She stiffened, locking her hands together to keep them from shaking.

"I would like to know precisely where we are going."

He slapped his gloves across his knee. "I was going to wait until we arrived, but if you insist . . ." He cleared his throat. "We are going to my country home to see my mother."

Constance was appalled. "Surely you jest. I'm not ready to meet your mother. I've sent no card. She has made no effort to call on us. Does she expect us?"

Jeremy made a feeble attempt to hide his laughter at her confusion. "No, she is not expecting us, but she will receive us nevertheless."

Constance was seething. She leaned forward, her face barely inches from his face. "Why are you doing this to me, Jeremy? You knew how angry I'd be."

"Better anger than indifference. For over a week now I've been trying to get through to you. I've wanted to explain things, but you've refused to listen."

Constance pressed her lips together in a thin line and settled back against the seat. After a while, Millicent broke the silence.

"You mentioned that your mother has been ill. I trust that our untoward visit will not unduly distress the countess."

"My mother is stronger than she appears. It is true that she had a brief bad spell the other night. She has occasional spells but usually recovers within minutes. Last time took longer than we expected. It's her heart, you know."

Constance didn't believe a word of it.

Wrightwood, the St. James country estate, was pure seventeenth century with a flat-topped, steeply pitched roof punctuated with attic dormer windows. Above this, on the main wing, were tall chimney stacks, a turreted cupola in the centre of the roof and a wooden balustrade running around the rim of the roof. A wide staircase led to the rather narrow entranceway, which was topped by a fan-shaped plaster facade. Tall trees set at a distance did little to soften the rigid exterior. Constance wondered if the Countess of Wrightwood would be equally uninviting.

Even before the three of them had reached the top step of the grand entrance, a butler and four footmen were waiting to see to their needs. Jeremy spoke briefly to the butler, who ushered them into a small drawing room. Jeremy adjusted his starcher.

"If you will be so good as to excuse me for a few minutes, I will inform my mother that we have arrived and are waiting to see her."

Constance didn't know what to say, so she said nothing. After he had gone she turned to Millicent. "I trust I have you to thank for this unfortunate arrangement."

Millicent at first looked away, then lifted her chin in defiance. "I grant you that a small measure of responsibility falls to me. I venture to say, however, that I had no idea, none at all, that he would go so far as to bring you here."

"I would far rather face the gibbet than be presented so...so spontaneously to the Countess of Wrightwood in such an unseemly way. It is most distressing."

"Perhaps it is for the best. At least you are forced to face Jeremy instead of playing the wounded virgin."

Constance pulled a face and refused to pursue a subject that she found distasteful. She turned her attention to the splendour of the room in which they waited.

The ceiling was taller than those in most homes, rising through the second storey of the house. The coffers were divided into moulded and ribbed hexagons of gilded plaster, and the larger ones contained paintings of classical figures in grisaille. The shades of grey were repeated against bold crimson in the carpet, which was shot with gold thread in a geometric design. It was an austere room with spindle-legged tables and straight-backed chairs that seemed to be designed for looking at rather than sitting.

Constance was nervous. It was all she could do to keep from wringing her hands. Then the door opened and Sir Jeremy reappeared.

He bowed. "If you would come with me, Lady Constance, my mother would like to speak with you."

Millicent put her hand on Constance's arm. "Would you like me to go with you, dear?"

"I . . . no, it isn't necessary. I'll not be gone long."

Jeremy grasped the front of his waistcoat. "Perhaps you would like to view the scroll collection in the library, Miss Seaforth."

Constance knew her aunt hated scrolls or manuscripts but she heard her say, "Yes indeed. I'd be pleased to see them."

Jeremy nodded to a footman who stood in attendance at the door. He snapped to attention and directed Millicent down a wide hallway that was decorated with huge tapestries.

"Are you sure your mother is well enough to have company?" Constance asked.

Jeremy, leading the way to a wide, curving staircase, looked thoughtful. "She's well enough now, though as I mentioned, she gave us a fright the night of the Regent's Ball." He gave Constance a significant look, then continued, "Of late she has taken to staying in her rooms, but she is not feeble. I would say that she is frail, being given to sudden vapours and occasional chest pains, but of course one must consider her age.''

"I do feel that I am imposing, calling on her without notice.''

"Nonsense. She demanded to see you—once she knew you were here.''

Constance lifted her eyes to the ceiling. "Once she knew I was here? Oh, Jeremy. You have a penchant for putting me in awkward positions.''

He started to say something, then shrugged. "Here we are.'' He knocked and opened the door without waiting for a response.

The bedchamber was nearly as large as the small drawing room they had used downstairs. It took a while for their eyes to become accustomed to the dim light. Heavy draperies blocked the sunshine from the row of windows that ran along one side of the room. A candelabrum flickered on a table near the bed, which sat on a raised dais.

Constance felt her gaze drawn like a magnet to the figure enthroned beneath the lace-and-satin canopy of the four-poster. The woman was of considerable age. Her hair, silver white and abundant, curled softly around a face so finely drawn that the traces of veins beneath the skin of her cheeks resembled fragile blue spiderwebs.

Jeremy made the introductions and smiled widely. "Was I not right when I said she was beautiful, Mother? What I didn't tell you is that she is also an artist.''

Constance was apparently not the only one aware of his forced charm. When he appeared to be about to continue, his mother frowned. "You have no need to prompt me, Jeremy. Shoo. Leave us alone. Shoo." She waved him off with a hand that reminded Constance of aging parchment.

Then the countess lay back against the embroidered pillows and reached for her quizzing glass. Her voice was surprisingly strong.

"So you're the one."

"I beg your pardon?"

"You're the one that half of London is abuzz over. What have you done to my son, girl? For three days he's been so muzzy-headed I thought he'd been struck in the head." She reached for her fan and fluttered it in front of her face. "Speak up now."

"I have no knowledge of what you speak. I only know that Lord Jeremy and I have attended routs together—always with the accompaniment of my chaperon and aunt, Millicent Seaforth."

"Indeed? You know, of course, that my son, if not officially engaged, is expected to marry Lady Francine Stropshire."

Constance was nettled. "It has nothing to do with me, I assure you. Perhaps it is Lord Jeremy whom you should remind of his obligations."

"Oh, fiddle. He knows his own business. It is you who must be told the way things are. I would hate to see you get hurt, young woman, though I daresay you've had your share of misfortune, considering your age."

"Toadflax!" Constance said with no little vehemence. "I am quite happy with my age." She saw the deepening lines of calculation around the woman's eyes. Constance smiled. "Are you trying to intimidate me, Your Ladyship? Because if you are, you're wasting your time."

A dimple flashed in the woman's chin. "Cheeky, aren't you? You're not from around these parts. Just where did you chance to meet my son?"

Constance drew a deep breath. Here was a conundrum. If she told her about The Tart Shoppe it might bode ill both for her and for Jeremy. If she lied and the countess already knew... She tucked her hands in the sleeves of her dress and weighed her words.

"The fact of the matter is I had fallen quite ill from a bit of pigeon pie I'd consumed at an inn. Sir Jeremy happened to find me unconscious and saved my life."

The woman pursed her lips and rested her head back on the pillow. "So. You have chosen to make a hero of him."

"Indeed not. I simply told you the truth."

"Huh. And where was this place he found you?"

"A little place just outside of London. My aunt and I were on our way to the city from Cornwall, where I used to live."

"And does this little place have a name?"

Drat! Constance thought. *She'll have it her way or no.* There was no doubting Jeremy was this woman's son. A pox on both of them!

"I am waiting, Lady Constance."

"I consider it rude of you to pursue this line of questioning when it must be clear that I prefer not to speak of it. If you must know, the name of the inn was The Tart Shoppe."

"Ah, yes. Madame Arabella Duprey's elegant little bordello. Forgive me, Lady Constance. I merely wanted to see if you found it easy to lie. Apparently you don't. My son told me much the same story."

"So be it!" Constance snapped. "If there is nothing else you wish to quiz me about, I would like to take my departure."

"Sit down. There is much we have to say to one another."

And sit down Constance did for the next hour or more. Before she was dismissed the woman had extracted her life story as well as the information that it was her hope and dream to have children before she reached her dotage.

At length, the countess reached for her hand. "My dear, you must know that Jeremy cares deeply for you. I do admit that if it were my choice he would marry Lady Francine. She is a spoiled chit, but it would be a splendid match considering she stands to inherit the lands adjoining our estate. However, I suppose you'll do. I shall see that Jeremy understands."

Constance was not flattered. "I fear it will take more than his understanding to pave the way to our betrothal. I'm not at all certain I care to further my relationship with your son."

The countess cut loose with an unladylike peal of laughter that was sure to have been heard below-stairs. "A creditable attempt, my lady, but hardly believable. I saw the look in your eyes when he was here in this room. Now off with you. We'll talk again before the banns are posted." She gave a yank on the bell-pull and a footman appeared to escort Constance downstairs.

Jeremy and Aunt Millicent were both waiting in the drawing room. Jeremy stood and approached her. "Was that my mother who was laughing?"

"She has a perverse sense of humour."

Jeremy beamed. "Great heavens! I haven't heard her laugh in over a year. What did she say to you?"

"Nothing that bears repeating. I would like to go home now, if you would be so good as to inform your driver."

"I was hoping you would stay the night."

"No, thank you."

"It is getting late, you know, and the roads are dangerous after dark."

"Then I suggest you remain safely behind."

He swore softly. "Very well. I'll see you home, but first I must arrange for outriders." He nodded to the butler. "There will be time for light refreshments before we are ready to leave."

Millicent was all in a dither with questions about Jeremy's mother, but Constance was not ready to share her thoughts, particularly not in the forbidding presence of the butler and the overzealous servants. Constance was aware that she was receiving more than her share of scrutiny. Had word already spread along the servant grapevine that she had received the blessing of Lord Jeremy's mother? Of course it had. Servants were always the first to know.

It seemed an eternity before the carriage was brought around with its complement of four armed outriders to ensure their safety. Highwaymen had become a fact of life as the distance between the economic classes grew wider. Although Constance hated the need for protection, she was grateful that they could ride after dark in comparative safety.

The darkness within the carriage provided for chicanery of another sort. They had not been on their way for more than ten minutes when Constance felt Jeremy's ankle rub against hers. She looked across at him, a sharp reprimand on the tip of her tongue, but he seemed oblivious to the fact that he was touching her.

The devil take him, she thought. How could he be so damnably unaware of her when his mere touch sent sparks of fire through her limbs? She knotted her hands together to keep them from shaking.

She waited, but he didn't move. She cleared her throat. "Am I crowding you, my lord? Do you have enough room?"

He looked at the empty seat on either side of him and grinned. "Oh, quite! And you, Miss Seaforth? Is there enough room with the two of you seated on the same bench?"

Millicent yawned. "I'm quite comfortable, thank you, but I must confess to being sleepy. Hot cocoa always does that to me."

She spoke the truth because a few short minutes later she was sound asleep. Her head leaned toward Constance, crowding her more than usual.

Jeremy grinned. "There is plenty of room over here, should you care to join me."

"I would rather die first."

"Never mind. We have plenty of time to be together. You'll get used to it."

"I don't know what you are talking about."

"Of course you do. I'll wager my mother made it very clear. I plan to marry you."

"And I suppose I have nothing to say about it?"

"Only if the answer is yes."

"And what will you do about it if the answer is no?"

"The question will never arise."

She laughed. "You are incorrigible. Fortunately I am well aware that you do not always follow through on your boasts."

"On that I must protest. When did I fail to do as I promised?"

"When you said you would return for me at the Regent's Ball."

"Ah, but I did return. You had already taken your leave."

"Had I waited, our host would have been forced to charge me room and board."

He shook his head. "Come now, Lady Constance. You must find a better argument than that. I always keep my promises."

She reached over and prodded him in the chest with her forefinger. "Do you indeed? Then how about your promise to introduce me to the Prince Regent? A mere invitation to dine at Carlton House does not suffice."

Jeremy captured her finger in his palm and held it securely. "Be careful, Lady Constance. You tread on thin ice." He lifted her hand to his lips and kissed each finger, one by one by one.

CHAPTER ELEVEN

THEY HAD NO SOONER stepped inside the door at The Beeches than Stavers presented Constance with a perfumed, gold-embossed missive bearing the seal of the Prince of Wales himself.

Millicent was beside herself with eagerness. "Do hurry and open it, child," she urged. "Lord Jeremy and I are dying of curiosity."

Constance opened it carefully, never once taking her gaze from Jeremy, who looked like a cat who has lapped up the cream.

"I have the feeling Jeremy already knows what it says," Constance said. She scanned it quickly, then handed it to Millicent.

"Great lackaday! An invitation to spend the week's end at the Royal Pavilion in Brighton as personal guests of the Regent." Millicent all but threw her arms around Jeremy. "We have you to thank for this, no doubt. However did you manage it, Lord Jeremy?"

Constance laughed sharply, giving him no opportunity to respond. "Lord Jeremy holds the lofty notion that he can do anything he sets his mind to."

Millicent giggled and clasped her hands before her face. "I can well believe that, my dear. And why not?

I like a man who does things. Lord Jeremy, I'll wager you never fail to get your own way."

Jeremy gave Constance a significant look, then returned his gaze to Millicent. "It would seem I have a penchant for achieving meaningless goals, Miss Seaforth. Getting what I *really* want appears to take considerably longer."

Millicent removed her bonnet and touched her hair. "I'm sure your ambitions are most admirable."

"As is your conceit," Constance murmured, so low that only Jeremy could hear.

Millicent moved closer. "What did you say, Constance?"

Jeremy slapped his gloves across his thigh. "I believe she said, 'And he never retreats.' I confess, Her Ladyship knows me far better than I presumed."

Constance shot him a dark look. "You presume too much as it is. I suggest you take your departure, sir, before you learn the true meaning of the word 'retreat.'"

He bowed. "As you wish. Remember, though, this is only a skirmish, not the war." He pulled on his gloves, smoothing them over his hands. "Until tomorrow, then."

"Tomorrow?" Constance searched her mind for a forgotten engagement.

Millicent provided the answer. "Oh, dear. I neglected to tell you that I promised Lord Jeremy we would receive callers at three. I trust that you have no objection."

Constance studied the smug look on Jeremy's face. "Objection? Why should I object? He has my per-

mission to court you, Aunt Millicent. It is my understanding that he leans toward mature women. As for
myself, I expect to be indisposed.''

Jeremy laughed. "I would hope your indisposition
will change for the better. For now, I'll bid you good-
night.''

There was no putting a bridle on Millicent once
Jeremy had gone. She trotted from one room to another, oblivious to the fact that it was well past the
hour for retiring.

"What a stroke of luck we had when you chanced
to eat that pigeon pie. My dear! Can you imagine?
Two whole days at the Royal Pavilion. Had they asked
I would have given ten years of my life for such an
opportunity.''

Constance ceased brushing her hair and observed
her aunt's reflection in the mirror. "I only hope we
don't live to regret it. I wonder who else is on the guest
list.''

Millicent sobered. "You're thinking of Lady Francine, I daresay. I do hope we will be spared that inconvenience.... Dear heaven! It just occurred to me.
Whatever shall we wear?''

Finding the answer would take the better part of the
next few days.

TRUE TO HIS WORD, Jeremy called the following day.
His behaviour was circumspect, and Constance, try as
she might, could find no fault with him. He took pains
to answer each and every question Millicent put to him
concerning their stay at the Brighton Pavilion. Moreover, he insisted they make the four-hour journey there

in his carriage. Every argument Constance put forth only made it clear that he was determined. In the end she relented, telling herself that she was doing so for Aunt Millicent's sake.

A whirlwind trip through the shops to select fabrics was followed by a wearisome week of stitchings and fittings with a pair of dressmakers who took over a suite of rooms on the top floor at The Beeches.

Millicent discovered an amethyst velvet, which she was having made into a panniered gown embroidered at the top with pale pink roses. Constance chose a heavy silk in antique ivory. The gown was simple to the point of severity, with its Empire design, scalloped neckline and a sheer, cutaway overdress of shimmering blue-green tulle. Even she agreed, when the final thread was knotted, that the full effect was breathtaking.

At the last minute she found a pair of silk slippers in an identical shade of blue green at a shoemaker's tiny shop in the rear of a drapers on Leicester Square. The price was outrageous, but Millicent assured her it was a "good investment." Constance didn't bother to ask her to explain her choice of words.

In spite of all her efforts to remain calm, Constance was excited by the prospect of the journey to Brighton. Jeremy invaded her thoughts more frequently than she would have liked. Indeed, he was becoming something of an obsession against which she was unprepared to do battle. But whenever she was tempted to consider the thought of marriage to Jeremy, she reminded herself of what her mother and stepmother had been forced to endure, thanks to her philandering father. Considering Jeremy's past, it was unlikely that he would cut his ties with others who lived the Corinthian life.

The morning of their departure arrived all too soon to suit her. She needed more time to build her defenses against Jeremy's relentless pursuit. But Millicent, having scarcely closed her eyes the night before, was waiting with her portmanteau and valises already packed when Constance went downstairs for her cup of chocolate.

Less than an hour later Constance heard Jeremy's carriage enter the gravel drive. She moved to a window and watched from behind slightly parted curtains.

The devil take him, he was a handsome man. Doeskin trousers fit snugly beneath a black waistcoat and fawn-coloured shirt of ruffled silk. He doffed his cloak and left it on the carriage seat before he swung energetically up the stairs to the entrance.

Constance went back to her dressing table and surveyed herself in the mirror one last time. She chewed her lip. Should she have worn the blue travelling dress instead of the moss green? She glanced at the clock. There was no time to change now. Why did she feel so...? She shook her head, unable to pinpoint just what it was she did feel. Uncertainty and frustration? Given the least reason she would have excused herself and stayed behind, but she knew Jeremy too well to think he would give her any opportunity to dissemble. And it was already time to depart.

When Jeremy saw Constance coming down the stairs in her travelling cloak he was puzzled and disappointed by her lack of enthusiasm. She had made no secret of her desire to meet the Prince of Wales. To be invited as a house guest at the Brighton Pavilion should have been one of the high points of her life. Yet she looked so forlorn. He wanted to take her in his arms and promise to make everything right, but he was more than a little afraid it was mainly his presence that disturbed her. For the first time in his courtship of her he was beginning to have doubts.

His doubts continued until they had travelled several miles along the Brighton Road. If Constance was unusually quiet, Millicent made up for it. She sat on the edge of her seat the better to aim her quizzing glass at everything and everyone along the way.

"Can you believe it? The road is so smooth. I still remember the holes our carriage encountered on the way up to London from Cornwall."

Jeremy drew his attention away from Constance with considerable effort. "If the Regent hadn't discovered the healing powers of the sea air, Brighton would be as difficult to reach as Cranmere Pool in the middle of Dartmoor. They say it used to take fourteen hours from London to Brighton. Now we can make the fifty-three miles in four hours, with a stop at the village of Crawley."

They ceased talking for a few minutes when a barouche-and-four careered around their carriage, followed by a high-sprung phaeton pulled by a pair of wild-eyed roans. The driver, wearing bright yellow pantaloons, was well into his cups. They weren't the first such vehicles to rattle by in a headlong race.

Constance raised herself from a self-imposed melancholy long enough to register curiosity. "Where is everyone going in such a rush?"

Jeremy eased his long legs to a more comfortable position, being careful this time not to brush against her.

"By tomorrow morning you might count a hundred or more gigs on the road. This route to Brighton passes near Crawley Downs, where the latest bout of fisticuffs between Cribb and Molineaux is to take place tomorrow afternoon."

Constance shuddered. "I'm surprised that you don't plan to attend. Pugilists and dog fights seem to be the sort of thing that would pique your interest."

He gave her a smouldering look. "That may have been true at one time, but now there are other things closer at hand to whet my thirst for adventure."

Constance blushed, as he apparently hoped she would. Millicent missed the veiled exchange and jumped right in. "I understand that you have expressed an interest in promoting the cause of the farmer. Is it true that you have put in your bid to address Parliament on the subject?"

He inclined his head and smiled. "You have heard correctly. When this great event shall take place I've yet to learn, but suffice it to say that I deem it an honour. I only hope that my words will be strong enough to bring about a movement to repeal the Corn Laws."

Constance was both surprised and impressed. "I had no idea you were actively involved in working for reform. I thought it was only a sham."

"Indeed. Could it be that you don't know me as well as you thought you did, Lady Constance?"

"We shall see, shan't we?"

He grinned and slowly relaxed until his knee brushed hers. She gave him a swift look and rolled her eyes in the direction of the ceiling. There was no getting around him. He was hopeless.

They stopped at the Inn of the Golden Harp for a brief repast and to freshen themselves and their horses. The inn was plastered with daub and wattle to the high oaken beams and the quarried windows. A crowd of men jostled one another, all of them gabbling at once over the bout of fisticuffs that was to take place the next day between the two boxers.

When Jeremy's carriage left Crawley they were two-thirds of the way to Brighton. Millicent dozed off almost immediately, but Jeremy was not inclined to sleep, nor was Constance. She made space to avoid further contact with his wayward knee, but to no avail. At one point he moved away and Constance suddenly felt a great sense of loss. She hated weakness. A sigh escaped involuntarily.

Jeremy, ever quick to note her changes of mood, leaned forward. "Is something bothering you, Constance?" he whispered in order not to waken Millicent.

Constance fixed her gaze on his hand and smiled sweetly. "Why, nothing at all, my lord. What could possibly be bothering me?"

He grinned. "I thought perhaps you might be a trifle warm?"

"If I am, you may rest assured I shall simply remove my cloak."

"And I shall be here to help you."

"I can manage quite well, thank you."

He smiled. "She was right, you know."

"Whatever are you talking about?"

"My mother. She said you appeared dangerously independent."

"Dangerously? What a strange word to use. Besides, should it chance to be true, it is hardly a concern of yours."

He chuckled. "I think she meant dangerous in the respect that you would be hard to handle, therefore a threat to our happy marriage."

"Give her credit. To be warned is to be armed. I suggest you would be wise to look elsewhere for a wife."

He shook his head, and his voice was low and husky when he spoke. "No, Constance. Whether you admit it or not, you were spoken for the first time I laid eyes on you at Madame Duprey's. Take my word for it, my love, I can handle you."

His words created vivid pictures in her mind, pictures that no decent woman would allow to enter her head. Too unsettled to speak, she studied his face for a moment. Then she turned away quickly with the hope that he had not seen the sparkle of tears in her eyes.

They rode the rest of the way in silence. Both of them were deep in thought, yet at the same time keenly aware of each other's presence.

It was sometime later that Millicent awakened, looked out the carriage window and drew a sharp breath. She touched Constance's knee. "Look! There it is. The Brighton Pavilion. Isn't it magnificent?"

Constance was ill prepared for the strange architecture, though she had read of the palace's peculiar combination of Chinese, Indian and Moorish designs. "It is extremely unusual," she said cautiously. "I had no idea it was still being built."

Jeremy took the opportunity to lean his head close to hers. "You don't sound enthralled. Maybe you agree with the wit who said it looked as if St. Paul's Cathedral had come to Brighton and pupped."

Constance laughed. "It looks like something out of the Cinderella story, with its turreted domes, minarets and golden columns." She let her gaze sweep from the gravelled drives to the rolling green lawns to the colourful beds of flowers. "And yet there is a certain undeniable charm. As if a child told the architects what kind of palace to build."

Jeremy leaned back. "There are those who say the Regent is simply an overgrown child."

Constance protested. "Oh, you speak so cruelly of him. Have you no respect?"

"On the contrary. There is much to admire about the Regent. There is one report that says the Regent borrowed money to help out an officer when he returned from a campaign and was unable to support his family. He is a generous man and exceedingly charming. But that does not signify, because in many ways he has yet to mature."

Millicent lifted her nose. "They can say what they want but I admire the Royal Pavilion and I want to see every inch of it."

"Even the tunnels, Aunt Millicent?"

"The tunnels? You mean there really are tunnels under the palace?"

Jeremy stroked his chin. "You've been listening to too many rumours."

"What rumours?" Millicent demanded.

"Of illicit rendezvous between the Regent and young virgins."

Millicent looked shocked. "Please, my lord. Do guard your tongue."

"My apologies. I had no intention of elaborating. I only wished to point out that the tunnels are hardly begun. It will be ten years perhaps before they are completed." He drew his hand across his moustache. "I suspect it would be unwise to explore too far without an invitation from the Regent. As to the rumours, they are the product of idle gossip and completely without foundation."

Millicent was mollified. "I've no doubt you're right. To run true to form the Regent would be more likely to rendezvous with a grandmother."

They laughed despite themselves and were still smiling when they reached the palace grounds.

From then on it was a blur of activity. The moment the carriage arrived inside the gate, a corps of liveried footmen lined up to assist them to alight and arranged for their luggage to be sent to their respective rooms.

As expected, the Regent was nowhere in sight. His public appearances were few since he had lost his figure, as well as favour with the majority of his subjects, but he still loved to entertain.

Foster, the assistant butler, and a troop of four footmen and a ladies' maid escorted the women to their suite. Jeremy was to occupy a room at the opposite end of the corridor.

Despite the extravagant size of the palace, there seemed to be people everywhere. Constance queried the butler. "How many house guests are staying here?"

He inclined his head. "There will be seventy, Your Ladyship, including you and Miss Seaforth and Lord Jeremy."

"Seventy! I thought perhaps twenty."

Millicent laughed. "When you're a prince you entertain on a princely scale. Would you happen to know if Lady Francine Stropshire is among the invited?"

He bowed. "I regret to say, Miss Seaforth, that Lady Stropshire is not on the list."

Millicent grinned. "I assure you, Foster, *we* have no regrets."

The ladies' maid tittered and Foster tried without success to hide a smile, then he and the rest of the entourage left the women alone with a promise that their personal maid would return shortly to unpack for them.

Millicent put her hands on her hips as she walked from the black-and-gold lacquered armories to the Tang Dynasty urn that stood in one corner of the room. "I could close my eyes and swear I was in China

now. Yet from the Moslem designs on the outside of
the palace I thought the interior would have more of
a Persian or Indian motif.''

"From what little I know about it, Henry Holland
designed the main building, beginning with the Ma-
rine Pavilion, but then his pupil, P. G. Robinson,
added the two oval-shaped wings. I understand he was
the one responsible for the shell-like canopies over the
windows.'' Constance began to unbutton her dress.
"It was when the Regent was given some Chinese
wallpaper that he decided to do the interior in the
Chinese style.''

"Odd,'' Millicent said, running her fingers across
the tail of a gilt dragon. "But I thought John Nash
was the architect not Henry Holland.''

"I believe Nash is designing the altera-
tions...adding the new kitchen, which I understand
is to be steam-heated.''

"Can you imagine! No wonder Prinny is so flat in
the pocket.''

Constance threw her aunt a warning glance.
"Maybe we should change and go the drawing room
as the butler suggested.''

The maid returned a few minutes later to lay out
their clothing while they freshened themselves. Constance wore a pale pink muslin embellished with pink
silk roses and a high bodice. Millicent selected a black-
and-silver-trimmed grey velvet out of respect to the
lack of warmth in the rooms.

It took them some time to find the way through the
maze of corridors, which were lit by red-tasselled lanterns hung from the ornate ceilings or from gold stan-

dards anchored to the floor. Deep, ceiling-high niches held velvet-robed or silk-gowned statues of Chinese potentates. Exquisitely painted vases were set at intervals against bamboo-decorated wallpaper. To Constance, it was a feast for her artist's eye and she itched to have time to sketch.

When they reached the drawing room they found that Jeremy had preceded them and was now engrossed in conversation with half a dozen men. A servant brought a tray of sherry to Millicent and Constance. They each took a glass and soon melded into separate groups of house guests.

Constance joined a circle of women, acquaintances for the most part. Lady Chatfield, the Countess Lieven, Miss Penelope Stanley and the Duchess of Heatherwood, whom Constance admired greatly. They were discussing the latest styles in *La Belle Assemblée*. She endeavoured to follow the somewhat dull conversation, but her gaze kept drifting around the room.

It was more of the classic style, cool and uncluttered. Tall windows lined two of the walls, with draperies held back by gold swags at table height. Chairs were placed in conversational groupings set off by rectangular Wilton rugs in a flowered pattern. A tall column entwined with some sort of plaster decoration and topped by a tasselled canopy hindered her view and she moved slightly to the left. As she did so, she saw Jeremy on the other side of the hall. She felt her colour rise. Had he supposed she was searching the room for him?

He smiled and inclined his head as if to say he knew what she was thinking. She looked away, but the intensity of his gaze drew her eyes like a magnet, and she looked back. This time she determined it was *he* who would be forced to lower his eyes first.

Jeremy saw the defensive lift of her chin and couldn't help smiling. He had been looking for her for the past twenty minutes; if she had taken longer he would have gone searching for her on the pretext that she might have lost her way.

Indeed, he thought sadly, it was he who had been lost from the moment he first saw her. He loved her independent ways; they both intrigued and infuriated him. But she was also a woman of great beauty, intelligence and compassion.

His mother had approved of her, though somewhat reluctantly. In the face of his advancing age and failure to produce an heir, the countess saw the handwriting on the wall and admitted that, with her breeding, Constance would make an acceptable match. It was just as well. He had every intention of wedding her, with his mother's approval or not.

The exchange of glances between Constance and Jeremy continued across the crowded room. She made a feverish attempt to submerge herself in animated conversation, but her gaze kept returning to meet his against her will. He was enjoying himself, she had no doubt, but she was becoming thoroughly annoyed by her own childish lack of control.

Jeremy had finally made his way to Constance's side when it was announced that the Regent was about to join them in the banqueting room.

There was a sudden flurry of activity, a heightened sense of awareness, as each man found the lady whom he was assigned to escort to the table. It came as no surprise to Constance that she was expected to take Jeremy's arm.

She looked around for Millicent, simply to make sure she was well cared for. Her aunt was standing near a long, low table with curved ends, and at first Constance thought she was quite alone. But as she watched, a tall, balding man of dignified stature approached Millicent and bowed. He was rather handsome, though no longer young. He inclined his head close and said something to her. Millicent stepped back, seeming to require the support of a nearby pillar.

Before Constance could make a move to go to her, the gentleman took Millicent's arm in his and she appeared to recover.

Constance leaned toward Jeremy. "Who is that man speaking to Aunt Millicent?

He looked surprised. "Oh, I say. He's Frederick, Duke of York."

"The Prince's eldest brother?" Constance was astounded.

"Indeed. I hadn't realized he would be here. He's out of favour, you know, since the Mary Anne Clark scandal."

"I didn't know."

"Quite. She was his mistress some years back while he was in the Military. But there was a Parliamentary enquiry and she was caught selling commissions and such. Frederick lost his commission, but the Regent was so devoted to him he made him commander-in-chief again."

"Did he marry her? His mistress?"

"Not likely. He married a German princess, but it didn't last. She's living in Surrey with a houseful of dogs."

Constance studied her aunt's face as she looked up at the man next to her. And suddenly Constance knew beyond any possible doubt that the duke was the lost love for whom Millicent had grieved all those long years.

CHAPTER TWELVE

SEEING AUNT MILLICENT'S obvious distress at meeting the duke was disturbing, but Constance had no time to consider the situation and its possible consequences. She and Jeremy were caught up in the procession of guests being directed to the banquet hall.

There was a babble of congeniality mixed with the excitement of dining with the future King of England. Constance would have gladly forgone the honour just to be alone with Jeremy. She needed his strength, however, and at this moment, at least, it seemed so right for them to be together. Yet, at the same time, Constance knew she was courting disaster.

Jeremy chose not to make it easy for her to ignore him. With his right hand, he reached over and covered her hand, which rested demurely on his left arm. She glanced up at him, ready to properly set him down, but the expression on his face was so tender that she could only smile and look away.

They had only just been seated at the huge table, with its fine linen cloth, heavy silver and thin porcelain service plates, when the Regent's arrival was announced and they all stood.

Constance tried not to crane her neck. Since they were seated according to rank, she and Jeremy were a good distance down the table, but she managed a glimpse. The Prince Regent looked rotund and jovial, not regal in any sense of the word; but even from this distance she saw his brilliant blue eyes and knew they could captivate an audience if he chose to do so.

Jeremy saw her obvious interest and said, "Don't worry. You will be presented to Prinny after dinner."

"Oh, Jeremy. Do you think so?"

He levelled his eyes at her, but before he could say anything, she gave in. "All right. You've made your point, sir."

The Prince motioned the guests to sit down while he remained standing. When everyone had been seated by a footman in attendance behind each chair, the Regent gave a brief welcoming speech, which charmed everyone present.

And then began the parade of food. One was expected to sample everything. There were four soups, and one was potato. In fact, potatoes and wine were served with each of the thirty-six courses except dessert, a deliberate and expected repetition.

Constance took exceedingly small portions and still found herself pushing the food around on her plate rather than eating it. She was entranced by the magnificence of the room with its massive crystal-and-gilt chandeliers with gold dragons, whose up-curved tails held lotus-blossom lights. They were suspended from chains attached to a gold starburst, which fastened to a column held in the claws of a winged monster with the head of a bird and the tail of a snake. This in turn was centred on a circle of dusky green palmate leaves made of some exquisite metallic enamel. The overall effect was highly dramatic and surprisingly artistic.

The Chinese influence dominated the entire room, which was decorated in gold and crimson. It occurred to Constance that after a while so much gilt and glitter was like too much food. One began to yearn for the more subtle gleam of polished wood carved in simple, classic lines.

The meal took forever. There were many moments of enjoyable conversation with the couple on either side of them. The elaborate centrepieces of fruits and flowers prevented conversation across the table. Jeremy seemed content to talk to Constance, and in truth, she enjoyed talking to him for once without challenging or being challenged at every other word. She was pleased to see him on his good behaviour. And admittedly, she treated him less caustically than she was wont to do. Perhaps the food had lulled them into a semiconscious state, she thought, then smiled.

He looked approvingly. "I see you've begun to enjoy yourself."

"How could I not? The Regent has made every effort to please us." She lowered her voice. "I must admit I'm a little worried about Aunt Millicent."

"She looked perfectly fit to me, although she did admit to being drowsy when she asked to be excused from dinner."

"If my suspicions are correct, she once had an assignation of some sort with the Duke of York. It was many years ago, of course, but she's still affected by it."

"Are you quite sure it was he?"

"No, but instinct tells me it was, and I am concerned about her."

"You think they are together, is that it? His Grace did cause a bit of a commotion when he spilled the wine on his waistcoat and left the table so abruptly."

"I think spilling the wine was a deliberate gesture."

"We can't leave the table until the Regent does, but as soon as we can, I'll help you look for your aunt."

"You're very kind. It won't be easy to find her in this crush."

"Try not to worry. Miss Seaforth is quite able to take care of herself. In some ways she reminds me of my mother."

Constance suppressed a groan. How could warm and loving Aunt Millicent ever be compared to his ogre of a mother?

He read her thoughts. "I know. My mother would seem somewhat of a tyrant to an outsider, but it is only out of the need to protect her family. Once you are one of us you will see the change in her."

Constance tried to keep the edge off her voice. "How long do you intend to continue this farce?"

"As long as necessary. Until you relent and agree to become my wife."

She was saved from responding by the soft chime of a gong. The room grew quiet and the Regent's aide made ready to remove his chair. Everyone rose. The Regent adjusted the heavy gold chain that encircled his considerable girth.

"If the ladies would care to adjourn to the drawing room, the gentlemen will join them within the hour."

Again the mass exodus through the maze of chinoiserie to the drawing room. One of the ladies who had visited the Pavilion on several occasions described the fabulous stables, the gardens, and the astonishing Chinese passageway of painted glass decorated with flowers and birds and illuminated from without. Constance was intrigued and looked forward to seeing it.

But more than that, she wanted to find Aunt Millicent, who was nowhere to be seen. It was unlike her to leave Constance unchaperoned, though they both knew that job was really only to keep up appearances.

The Prince, who was known to be undependable when it came to keeping appointments, was for once true to his word. It was in fact less than an hour that the gentleman, replete with port and the odour of tobacco, returned to the drawing room. A hush settled on the small group of women to whom Constance was telling a story. She thought they were merely being polite, until one of the women touched her arm, at the same time looking over her shoulder.

Lord Jeremy was standing there. Directly to his right was the Prince Regent.

Constance turned to face him and dropped a curtsey. After that, all she could remember was how the Regent had kissed her hand and told her that the Duchess of Heatherwood had given him his likeness that Constance had drawn the night of the party at Carlton House. He was pleased and begged to keep it in order to frame it for his library.

From that moment on, nothing she did was considered ordinary. Everyone tried to speak to her. The hostility she had encountered from a few people, mostly friends of Lady Francine, had vanished as if it had never been.

Jeremy, when he could manage to get to her side, took her hand in his and held it between his palms. "There now. Did I not promise the Regent would speak to you?"

She looked up at him with excitement shining in her eyes. "Sometimes you amaze me, my lord."

"What's more, I've found your aunt."

"Where? Is she all right?"

"Perfectly fit. She was being shown the stables by the Regent's brother."

"The stables? Millicent hates horses."

"Ah, but does she hate the duke?"

Constance furrowed her brow. "I don't know. I truly don't know."

The first opportunity Constance had to speak to her aunt was after they retired to their adjoining rooms. Constance entered Millicent's dressing room and sat down on a stool near the vanity table. She fixed her aunt with an accusing glare.

"You had me worried, you know. Who is the Duke of York that he could spirit you off like that, with not a word to anyone?"

Millicent's gaze slid away from hers. "Great lackaday! Such a fuss over nothing. Now you know, child, what it's like for me when you disappear from a party and I'm supposed to be watching you."

"You sound as if it has happened often."

She smiled. "Only when Jeremy St. James happens to be around. Have you decided to accept his offer of marriage?"

"I don't recall his having *asked* me. Lord Jeremy *tells* people. He doesn't ask."

"That comes naturally. He's descended from a long line of peers who are used to running things. I doubt that he's ever had to ask for anything in his life."

"Then it's time he learned." She studied her aunt's face. "And if you presume to put me off by asking questions instead of answering them, you are wrong."

"I don't know what you mean."

"It's the duke I'm asking about. You are so transparent, Aunt Millicent. When he approached you and bowed, it was obvious that it wasn't the first time you had met him."

"Indeed?"

"Was Frederick Augustus the man you were once in love with?"

Millicent busied herself at the armoire. "I have never discussed my private life with anyone, not even with my own mother. And I do not choose to discuss it now."

Constance was taken aback. Never had her aunt spoken so forcefully. "I'm sorry. I didn't mean to open old wounds. I only meant to help."

Millicent looked contrite. "And I didn't intend to sound so abrupt. I shouldn't have left you today. It was my responsibility to see to your chaperonage."

"Toadflax! I'm old enough to take charge of my own life."

Millicent tucked her hands in the sleeves of her gown and slowly paced the floor. "Then see to it that you don't let it slip through your hands the way mine did."

"You think I ought to marry Jeremy?"

"He's a fine man. One, I'll wager, who's sown his share of wild oats and is ready to settle down."

"I wish I could believe that. Does that mean I have your blessing?"

"If you want it. Do you?"

"I don't know. One part of me wants him more than I can say. The other part remembers how my father treated women, and I am afraid of repeating history."

"Jeremy St. James is not your father."

Constance dimpled. "For that I'm grateful at any rate."

"There comes a time in life, my dear Constance, when one must take a chance. I think you've had the courage and good sense to know when that time arrives."

They talked for a while, then Constance retired to her own room to think about what Millicent had said . . . and to think about what it would be like to be Jeremy's wife.

The following morning the guests feasted on a huge breakfast, which was laid out on sideboards in the refectory. Constance had wakened early, eager to see the sights and explore the garden. Millicent groaned at the early hour but readied herself to act the dutiful chaperon.

Predictably, Jeremy was waiting for them in the refectory. He speared a crusty pilchard with a fork. "I regret to tell you that I will be occupied for an hour or two today, the Prince would like to show off some of his prize horses. I hope you can find something to do."

Constance laughed. "I could easily occupy myself for a dozen hours. I want to draw everything. As for Aunt Millicent . . ."

Millicent ladled some honey onto a scone. "You've no need to concern yourselves with me." She shot a glance at Constance. "As long as I know my charge is behaving herself like a lady, I am content."

When they finished their meal, Jeremy took the women on a short tour of the south wing. It was there that Constance saw the Chinese corridor of painted glass, and she was enthralled.

She put out her hands and did a graceful pirouette. "It's unbelievable," she said. "With the light coming from the outside, it must be like being inside a gigantic Chinese lantern. I can't wait to start drawing."

Millicent pursed her lips. "To each his own, I daresay. As for me, I could do without the painted insects and birds, and I'll stay on the *outside* of my lanterns, thank you."

When it was finally time for Jeremy to go to the stables, Millicent decided to take a nap while Constance returned to the lantern corridor to sit with her sketch pad and pencils. Some of the guests had set up games of whist and faro, while others were strolling in the garden or relaxing in the library.

Constance was pleased to have the time alone, but try as she might, she could not bring herself to sketch the intricate and exotic Chinese designs. Each time she turned to a fresh page in her sketchbook, her hand of its own accord began drawing Jeremy's face. It wasn't the first time she had done so. Indeed, she thought, this book, like the others she had used up since coming to London, was full of him. She knew each angle and plane of his face and his form as if she had touched them individually with her fingers.

How long she had been there she didn't know, but suddenly she looked up and Jeremy was standing there watching her.

She closed her book with a snap. "You're the quiet one. I didn't hear you approach."

He inclined his head and moved closer. "I hated to disturb you. You looked so intense—and beautiful."

"Thank you. You're back sooner than we supposed."

"I brought a message. Your aunt would like to see you as soon as possible in her room."

Constance jumped up. "Is she all right? Is she ill?"

"I don't think she is ill. I think she merely wanted to speak privately with you."

"I must go at once."

He rose. "I'll come with you."

"No. Please. I'd rather go alone."

"If you wish. Will you come back here afterward?"

She furrowed her brow. "I will if I can. If Aunt Millicent is all right."

He watched her go, her anxiety reflected in her quick and certain step. The light from outside the Chinese corridor lay like a golden aura around her and he watched until she was out of sight. As he stepped backward to find a seat on the stone bench, his foot encountered something, and he bent down to pick it up. It was her sketchbook.

He hadn't intended to snoop at first, but as he waited, he idly thumbed the cover and the book opened. There staring back at him from the pages of the sketchbook was his own likeness, viewed from a dozen different angles. Through his critical eye, Jeremy decided the drawings were romanticized. His eyes weren't so large, his hair was not so black or so wavy, his jaw not quite so well shaped. In truth, he wasn't as good-looking as she had drawn him.

A slow smile spread across his face and his chest expanded with a surge of unbelievable joy. "Egad," he said aloud. "The woman loves me. What better proof could I ask?"

CONSTANCE WAS SO INTENT on reaching her aunt's side that she gave little thought to the curious glances of the people she passed in the corridors. Please don't let her be ill, Constance prayed. Whatever it is, it had to be serious for Millicent to summon her.

Constance knocked once on her aunt's door and then grasped the doorknob. It turned and Constance entered the small sitting room. "Aunt Millicent?" she called.

"In here."

Millicent was sitting in a straight-backed chair looking out the window. She didn't bother to turn when Constance entered and knelt beside her.

"What is it, Aunt Millicent? Are you all right?" It was obvious she wasn't, but she looked more distracted than ill. "What can I do?" Constance persisted.

Millicent cleared her throat, then looked at Constance. "It appears I have a decision to make." She lowered her gaze, then looked back toward the window.

"You were right, you know, when you guessed that Frederick Augustus was the man I once knew. It was...it was, oh, so many years ago. We were both young and very foolish." Millicent knotted her handkerchief in her fingers. "But he was so handsome and so gallant that, indeed, he swept me off my feet. And I confess I've never quite got over him."

There was a long silence. Millicent seemed to be lost in reverie.

Constance prompted. "And now you've seen him again. And?"

"And he wants me to go away with him." She turned toward Constance and laughed sharply. "Now isn't that absurd?"

"No indeed. Not if that's what you truly want."

Millicent noticed that the handkerchief she was holding was mashed into a ball. She spread it on her lap and folded it into a neat square. "He has had a difficult life, you know. They brought him up on charges of selling military commissions, but it wasn't true. It was that woman, Mary Anne Clark." Millicent made an expression of distaste. "He's well rid of her now, but of course there is the duchess. He doesn't see her since she moved to Oatlands with her dogs, over a hundred of them, Frederick says. He isn't keen on dogs."

Constance stood and walked to the foot of the bed, where she sat down. "Have you decided what you want to do?"

"There's no question, is there, all things considered? I still have you to look after."

"Indeed! You can't be serious."

"And why not? I promised your dear mother as well as your dear stepmother that I would look after you until such time as you marry or reach the age of twenty-six."

"But we both know that I can take care of myself."

"It's a question of appearances, as you well know."

Constance stood and paced the floor. "I'll not have you using me as an excuse. It's your turn, Aunt Millicent. You deserve to have a life of your own."

"You talk as if my life has been completely devoid of joy."

"Not at all. The two of us have had wonderful times together, so I know that isn't true." Constance returned to a table by the window and picked up an ivory elephant. She ran her finger over the smooth carving and felt it warm beneath her hand.

"You told me a few short hours ago that there comes a time when one must take a chance on happiness in order to experience life to its fullest. Doesn't the same apply to you?"

Millicent lifted her shoulder and let it fall. "The rules change when you get older."

"Perhaps. But won't you always regret it if you don't go with him?"

"I suppose I will, my dear. I'll regret it for the rest of my life."

"Then that's your answer, isn't it?"

"It's not quite so simple." Millicent rose, looking oddly refreshed. "Well, now. You go back to Jeremy. Will you extend my apologies to him for having inconvenienced him?"

"I can't leave when you're feeling like this. I want to stay with you."

"Nonsense. Go back to Jeremy. He needs you more than I do."

Constance laughed. "That's the most ridiculous thing I ever heard. Jeremy doesn't need me. He's entirely self-sufficient."

"Indeed. I shouldn't be too sure of that, my girl."

Constance shook her head in disbelief, refusing to pursue the subject. "I'll leave you now, Aunt Millicent, but I'll be back shortly. If you look for me I'll be in the Chinese corridor."

Millicent shooed her away and Constance returned to where Jeremy was waiting on the bench.

"I'm sorry to have been gone so long," Constance said. "Aunt Millicent simply needed someone to talk to. I think she will be all right."

Jeremy rose. "I'm relieved to hear it." He handed her the sketchbook. "You left this behind in your haste."

Constance took it, all the while studying his face. There was no doubt in Jeremy's mind what she was thinking. Had he looked at the sketches she had drawn of him? If she knew he had she would be distressed, for Constance had an overripe sensitivity about her own privacy. Jeremy made his face a blank and offered his arm.

"Would you care to stroll in the gardens, Constance?"

She sighed audibly. "That's kind of you. I'd like it very much." And as she moved off, her hand delicately resting on his arm, she was able for a brief while at least, to push aside the thoughts that tormented her.

THAT NIGHT she lay awake for a long time. It was never easy for her to sleep in a strange room. The smells were different; even the sounds were not the sounds she was used to hearing in her bedroom at The Beeches. And tonight the thoughts she'd forced away earlier had returned in full force.

Aunt Millicent, she knew, was still wrestling with her decision about the Duke of York. There was no easy solution for her, but it was something she had to decide for herself. Constance wanted her to be happy. She loved her aunt as much as she had loved her own mother and stepmother.

Constance had her own decision to make. For a while she tried to picture life without Jeremy, but it was too bleak to consider for long. But if she married him and he returned to his philandering ways... Then again, wasn't it better to know love for a time, no matter how brief, then never to know it at all? The reasons weighed strongly in Jeremy's favour, but it was still too soon to make up her mind.

She had just come to that conclusion when she sat up in bed, convinced that she heard someone crying. She got up and and walked barefoot to the door but there was no one there. Then she realized the crying was coming from Millicent's room. Her first impulse was to go to her; then common sense told Constance that Millicent would not choose to share her grief.

Time went by, perhaps an hour. The crying ceased. At length, Constance, wanting to reassure herself that Millicent was all right, opened the door to her aunt's room and found she had gone. Her bed had not been slept in.

Constance hesitated for only a moment before running back to her own room, where she opened her armoire and began throwing on her clothing. Interfering she might be, but she had to be certain that Aunt Millicent was unharmed. Had it not been for the crying, Constance might have given her own action second thought, but she had never once in all the time they had been together seen Millicent cry.

Constance did not take time to look at the clock, but it was obvious from the all-pervading silence that everyone must have retired.

Constance finished fastening the last button on her dress as she left her room, then stopped midstride to consider the maze of corridors that connected the various rooms of the Royal Pavilion. She hadn't the least idea where to look for Millicent. Was she off on some rendezvous with the duke? If so, where would they go? It was unlike Millicent to meet him in his private quarters. No, it would be some less obvious place. The stables? Not likely. The grooms and stableboys no doubt occupied the stable at night along with the horses. Besides, she had no idea how to find the stables. She had seen the huge dome that housed the Regent's prize steeds, but had no idea how to get there. She needed help.

She needed Jeremy. Without giving another thought to what the scandal mongers might say if she were seen alone with him at this time of night, she headed down the corridor to his room and knocked quietly on the door. There was no response.

"Please let him answer," she prayed softly. She knocked again. This time there was a murmured response and Jeremy, wearing a dark robe, opened the door. He raked his fingers through his hair.

"Constance! What is it? Is something wrong?"

"I...I don't know. It's Aunt Millicent. I heard her crying in her room a little while ago. Now her room is empty and her bed has not been slept in. I...must find her. Will you help me look for her?"

"Of course. Just let me get dressed. Come in and... No, dash it all. You'd better wait out there. I'll only be a minute."

CHAPTER THIRTEEN

ALTHOUGH IT TOOK Jeremy scarcely any time to get dressed, Constance fidgeted more out of concern for her aunt than out of fear that someone might see her waiting outside Jeremy's door. It was scandalous behaviour, to be sure, but at the moment she cared not a whit.

His door opened and he stepped out, dressed in fresh clothing complete with cloak. Constance looked surprised. "I hadn't thought to look outside."

"Do you have any idea where she might have gone?"

"She's with the duke, I've no doubt of that. As to where they might have rendezvoused, I have no idea."

"Would they have gone to his rooms, do you think?"

"Surely not. Aunt Millicent would not have compromised herself so completely. No. They would find another private place."

Jeremy cleared his throat. "Er...someplace quite private?"

Constance shot him a look. "Sir! You presume too much. When I said private, I meant where they could speak without being disturbed."

"I beg your pardon," he said, matching his stride to hers.

"As well you should. Where is it we are going? To the stables?"

"Yes. The duke is quite at home in the stables. He could find privacy there. Would you care to wait here? You'll be cold without a cloak."

"No. I'm going with you."

He whipped off his cloak and adjusted it around her shoulders. "There. That should serve you well."

Constance would have protested, but the feeling of his coat around her was almost like being in his arms. His scent was everywhere. It invaded her senses like some potent drug, blotting out everything but her awareness of him.

Jeremy mistook her giddiness for concern over Millicent, and he put his arm around her and drew her close. It never once occurred to Constance to protest.

Jeremy was jubilant, though he took great care not to show it. It pleased him that Constance fit well under the crook of his arm. She had forgotten to put a cap over her hair and it floated around her like a cloud of sea foam.

The great dome of the stables with its eight-foot cupola lay at a considerable distance from the main buildings. Jeremy was having second thoughts about taking Constance over the rough path, but she was determined. The darkness gave him cause to hold her closer.

Once inside the dimly lit building she could see the ornate doors of Moorish or Chinese design that enclosed the forty or so horse stalls. The cavernous effect of the dome and the semidarkness gave an eerie feeling to the place, and it seemed natural when Jeremy lowered his voice.

"Wait by the fountain," he ordered, motioning to the hexagon-shaped drinking fountain for horses set in the middle of the room directly beneath the apex of the dome.

There was no chance for argument, but before he was twenty feet away, they were approached by a sleepy stableboy.

"Wot ken I do for yer, guvner?" he asked, yawning.

"Have you seen the Duke of York tonight?"

"I ain't seen 'im, guvner."

Jeremy stroked his chin. "I wonder. Do you know who he is?"

The boy gave him a scathing look. "Know 'im? Why, me an 'im is chums, we is. I looks after 'is new colt, I does, but 'e ain't been 'ere since early on this morn."

"Thank you, lad," Jeremy said, flipping him a gold coin. The boy tested it between his teeth and grinned hugely.

Constance caught up with Jeremy. "Where do we look now?"

"I was hoping you might suggest something." He stroked his chin. "Let's investigate the library. There's a smaller one that might be just the place the duke would choose for an assignation." He touched her arm and directed her toward a side corridor. They had gone no more than a few feet when they saw someone come out of a room and quietly close the door before turning in the opposite direction.

Constance stopped. "Look. It's Aunt Millicent. I'm sure it is. Let's hurry."

Jeremy put his hand on her shoulder and turned her to face him. "Hold a minute before we do. Wouldn't it be wiser to see her to her room without letting her know we followed? If we accost her now it would only serve to embarrass her."

"Yes. Of course. Then we must be careful she doesn't see us."

Jeremy chuckled. "I doubt that she would recognize you in my cloak."

"Oh, dear. I had completely forgotten." It was a lie. She hadn't forgotten. It was only that she loved the feel of it around her and hated to relinquish it.

They followed Millicent until she entered her own bedchamber, then Jeremy slowed his pace. "Well, that takes care of that." He looked down at Constance in the pale glow of the gaslight hanging from the ceiling. "I suppose you have to go in now."

Constance saw the intensity with which he studied her face. "I suppose I must."

"It wouldn't do for you to be alone out here with me this time of night."

"No. It wouldn't do at all."

"Someone might say that I tried to kiss you."

She tried to keep her voice light, but there was an unaccountable huskiness when she spoke. "Indeed they might. You know how people love to gossip."

"Even when it's not true."

"I know."

His indigo eyes held her with their warmth. "Then wouldn't you say it might be worth the risk?"

"I . . . I would certainly say so."

He took her shoulders in his hands and gently drew her to him. His hands were shaking. She guessed that he was trying to restrain himself, and indeed, his lips brushed hers so lightly that it could have been a dream. She cupped the back of his head with her hand, letting her fingers stroke the thickness of his hair. He tensed and his mouth hardened against hers, sending an explosion of exquisitely compelling sensations along her spine.

His kiss deepened and a warning bell went off somewhere in a dark corner of her mind.

"Jeremy, please. No more." She spoke breathlessly. "I must go in now."

"So soon? We've hardly begun."

She laughed shakily. "I know. And that, sir, is the very reason I must say good-night."

He kissed her hand, lingering longer than was proper, though in truth she didn't want him to stop.

"Thank you for your cloak," she said, handing it to him, " and thank you for helping me find Aunt Millicent."

He bowed. "The pleasure was mine."

Her door had scarcely closed behind her when Millicent came through the door from her adjoining room.

"So there you are, child. I was worried sick. Where have you been?" she demanded.

Constance, unable to stop smiling, sank down on the edge of her bed. "Where indeed? I was worried about you. I summoned Jeremy and we went in search of you."

"Oh, dear. Then I must apologize, but as you see, I am quite unharmed."

"So I see. In truth, you seem quite refreshed. Am I to understand that you have made a significant decision?"

"I have."

Constance sat up. "Well . . . tell me. You are making me daft with your reticence. When are you going off with him?"

Millicent sank down into a chair and leaned her head back against the rest. "I have decided against it."

"But why? Why should you give up your chance at happiness?"

"Happiness? My dear, it suddenly occurred to me that I *am* happy. I have no desire to be at the beck and call of any man, let alone one who is a bit of a pompous oaf."

"Aunt Millicent!"

"Very well, I take that back. Frederick Augustus is a kind and jovial man, but he has become something of a martinet when it comes to politics. I'm done with him, after all these years, and now I plan to get on with my life."

"You sound so . . ."

"Happy? Yes, and a little flattered to think that the duke is still interested in me. But I'm also very weary and I would like to retire. We have a long journey home tomorrow."

They said their good-nights and Millicent returned to her room.

There was a brief assembly the following day when the Regent said goodbye to his guests. He kissed Constance's hand and thanked her again for the likeness she had drawn of him. He also kissed Millicent's hand and spoke with her for several moments in a very cordial fashion. Frederick Augustus lingered in the background long enough to draw Millicent aside and speak privately with her. Constance noted that Jeremy stood nearby in the event that Millicent might require assistance. It warmed Constance to know that he should be so protective.

The ride home was accomplished in too short a time because it meant saying goodbye to Jeremy. He saw them inside, then Millicent tactfully left them alone.

Constance walked him back to the front door. "I can't begin to thank you enough for an extremely lovely holiday. Brighton and the Prince were more, much more, than I could possibly have imagined."

"It was magnificent, wasn't it? Strange, isn't it, that all the royal pomp and ceremony never impressed me before now, but seeing it with you made the difference."

Constance lowered her gaze. He took her chin in his hand and lifted it. "Can you deny, Constance, that we belong together? We both have waited an inordinately long time to wed. Perhaps the reason is that we were waiting for each other." He put his hands on either side of her face and kissed her softly on the mouth. "My love, you must begin to think seriously about our marriage, because we are wasting precious time. And I tell you this, I will never give up, never! Not until you consent to be my wife."

She would have consented then and there, but she had to be sure that his offer for her was not a passing whim born out of a perverse desire for the unattainable. When it came to marriage, caution was not an easy habit to overcome.

It was two days later that the invitation arrived for a musical evening at Marlborough house. Although Constance had wearied of the constant parade of routs and parties and would have sent her refusal, Millicent made a dash to her armoire to begin planning something extravagant to wear. When Jeremy called upon Constance the same afternoon and she learned he would also be in attendance, the picture brightened. Furthermore, he again offered the use of his carriage, which was far more elegant than the somewhat musty carriage Constance had brought from Cornwall.

Marlborough House at the eastern edge of St. James Palace, was approached by way of a narrow passage from Pall Mall, through which a coach-and-six could barely squeeze. Jeremy told the women that Sarah, the Duchess of Marlborough, who had ordered the house built in 1709, had been at sword's point with Sir Robert Walpole. When he learned she was building the house he bought up all the adjoining land, thus keeping her from having a view and an entrance in keeping with her sense of importance.

Constance was impressed with the building's clean lines and lack of ornamentation. Jeremy told her that the Duchess of Marlborough had advised her architect, Sir Christopher Wren, that she hated all manner of grandeur in architecture.

The house was a rectangular block, two stories high, with small projecting wings. The dominant feature was the large niches designed to hold statuary, two on each floor of the wing extensions.

Millicent added her bit of gossip as they passed through the iron gateway. "I hear that the Duke of Marlborough brought the bricks back from Holland as ballast on his ship so that he would not have to pay the expense of import."

Constance was about to comment on the privileges of power when she chanced to look out at an approaching carriage. There was no doubt that the attractive woman with elegantly plumed hat was Lady Francine Stropshire.

Millicent apparently caught the look on Constance's face, and she reached over to squeeze her hand in reassurance.

Once inside they were ushered up to the first floor of the mansion, ladies to one side, gentlemen to the other, in order to dispose of their wraps and refresh themselves. Constance and Millicent were welcomed into the circle of women who were chatting about the fact that in a year or so the lease on Marlborough House land that the Duchess had received from Queen Anne was due to expire, and the land would revert to the Crown. There was some talk that it would be designated as one of the royal residences. With that on dit, there was general babble about when it would take place. Then suddenly the door opened and Lady Francine and her chaperon entered. The babble dwindled to a few titters.

Lady Francine was even more beautiful than usual. She saw Constance and stopped dead. Constance inclined her head.

"Good evening, Lady Francine."

"Good evening, Lady Constance." They regarded each other coolly, neither woman choosing to back down. Then Lady Smithfield saved the day by telling Constance that Lord Jeremy was enquiring after her. Lady Francine tossed her head so that her diamonds glittered outrageously and she continued on into the inner room.

Constance and Millicent followed Lady Smithfield's lead until they were away from the crowd. "Thank you for the message from Lord Jeremy, Lady Smithfield," Constance said. "It came at a strategic time."

Lady Smithfield laughed. "Precisely. I saw that the two of you were about to do battle to defend your territory. I hope you will forgive my little untruth, but I have no doubt that my godson really is wondering where you are." She fingered a long string of pale pink pearls. "You will probably find him in the drawing room. I'm told the concert is about to begin."

Jeremy had reserved chairs for them near the rear of the crowded assembly. "I'm afraid we'll find the music disappointing," he said. "Young Baronzini lacks some of the sparkle of better-known pianists, but he has heart."

Constance enjoyed the selections from the Mozart operas and the more light-hearted ballads. As Jeremy had predicted, a few of the elder guests nodded off, only to be prodded into attention by their companions.

When it was over, the guests began to take their leave, but Lord Jeremy and his party were invited to join their host and a few select visitors, about twenty in all, for a late collation of cold meats, cheese and fruit. Unfortunately, Lady Francine and her father were among those invited.

Sarah and Oliver Fagan were late arrivals and they were untitled, but since Sarah was remotely related to the duchess, they were also invited to join the more private party. Constance made room for them next to her.

As the guests finished their food and sipped glasses of a fine wine, Baronzini, a bit into his cups, returned to the piano to entertain himself. When there was a heavy lull in the conversation, the duchess brought out a drawing pad and pencils.

"Lady Constance, I know this is rather bold of me, but would you be so good as to draw for us?"

Constance hesitated briefly, then agreed. "What would you like me to draw?"

"A likeness," several voices chimed in unison. She looked at Jeremy.

He levelled his gaze at her. "Don't you dare. I saw the notebook full of the drawings you did of me. You made me look far too pretty."

Constance, regarding him with something akin to anger, lowered her voice so that only he could hear. "You had no right to spy on my sketchbook. You are entirely without morals, sir!"

For the life of him, Jeremy didn't know why he'd blurted out his confession then and there. He was taken aback by Constance's reaction and would have apologized, but she turned away to face those who had gathered around her.

"We all know," she said, "that Lord Jeremy is preparing his address on the plight of the farmer for the next meeting of Parliament."

They listened closely as they watched her pencil fly across the page in quick, sure strokes.

"A worthy cause, to be sure, and one that needs all of our support." Several people cheered, but she heard at least one grumble coming from the side of the room where Lady Francine and her father held court.

Lord Stropshire looked somewhat strangled as he took an overlong swallow of port wine. "It's the devil's brew you're stirrin' up when you talk of farm reform, my girl. And it's men's talk, too, not meant for pretty ladies to think about."

Constance finished the drawing and signed it with a flourish. She handed it to the Fagans, who began laughing and handed it to the Duke of Devonshire. Then people who could no longer wait to see what all the fun was about began crowding in.

Jeremy could hardly miss the fact that the laughter involved him, but it was several minutes before the caricature came around to him. When it did, he laughed more loudly than anyone.

For the caricature was of him. He took one look at Constance, who seemed to be having second thoughts.

"All right, my lady. You must admit that this evens things up. True, I yielded to temptation and looked through your sketchbook, but this...this..." He shook his head. "Words fail me."

There was no doubt the sketch was a likeness of Jeremy, but it was unlike anything they had seen. He was dressed in farmer's garb: scruffy fustians, a pitchfork in his hand, ears standing out like weather vanes from his touselled hair and a piece of straw hanging from his mouth. The look on his face belied the least evidence of any human intelligence.

Jeremy was not inclined to let Constance have the last laugh. He rose and bowed to address the party goers. "Ladies and gentlemen, I assure you that the cause of the farmers is not the work of the devil, as Lord Stropshire would lead us to believe. Thanks to intelligent and talented people who are working toward reform, people such as Her Ladyship—" he bowed toward Constance "—we are sure to see some changes for the better in the near future."

There was a stir of restlessness as if the crowd were disappointed with Jeremy's speech. Jeremy stood straighter. "And there are sure to be other changes. When I take Lady Constance to wife she will be so busy with our brood of a dozen or so children that she will have no time for drawing caricatures of her husband or anyone else."

There was an audible gasp, then a round of vigorous applause.

Constance was appalled. How dared he? Her face turned a bright pink as people surrounded them with their well wishes.

Lady Smithfield beamed. "What a grand surprise. I'm so pleased, my dear. There is no one I would rather have as a wife for my godson."

Constance sighed. "A surprise indeed! I fear that Lord Jeremy is bamming you. He is merely having fun at my expense."

"Then you are not betrothed?" several people asked at once.

"We are not betrothed," Constance said, loudly enough so that no one could misunderstand. She picked up the sketchbook and studied the caricature. "I think my lord is simply trying to even the score."

Jeremy inclined his head. "The betrothal, my friends, is a mere formality. I'll wager that in six months' time Her Ladyship not only will be my wife but will be well on her way to becoming the mother of my child."

Again the room resounded with laughter.

Constance knew that the only way out of the farce was to let them enjoy themselves.

She cleared her throat and motioned for silence. "Lord Jeremy has yet to learn that a wager cannot father a child."

The guests laughed and applauded, then turned toward Jeremy, eager for his rebuttal.

He didn't disappoint them. "Perhaps not the wager itself, my lady, but *I* shall be happy—nay, overjoyed—to die trying."

After that there was nothing she could say to get back at him. Indeed, he made such a show of bowing and kissing her hand that it was clear the onlookers loved him and his bold ways.

It was late when they left Marlborough House. Their host informed them that it was the best party he had ever given and he hoped to see them again soon. He winked at Jeremy. "And if you need a godfather for any or all of your offspring, do count me first."

They were no sooner in the carriage than Constance confronted him. "Well, now. You did it up properly tonight. I trust you are satisfied at making us the laughingstock of all London."

He reached for her hand. "They loved it, Constance, and they also loved you. Am I not right, Miss Seaforth?"

Millicent slowly let out her breath. "You do have a way with you. But yes, I'll have to admit they did enjoy your little exchange."

"Exchange!" Constance blustered. "I . . . you . . . it was more like a public slaughter." She pulled her hand away from him and leaned back against the carriage seat. "I warned you, Jeremy, not to embarrass me again. One of these days I'll make you pay for it."

Jeremy settled back and studied her face. He knew she was not nearly as angry as she pretended to be. Between the two of them, they were going to make beautiful children.

CHAPTER FOURTEEN

WORD OF JEREMY'S DETERMINATION to wed Lady Constance spread through London like fire in a pitch barn. For two days she was bombarded with callers and messages. The stories people heard and passed on had become so distorted that some thought the date had been set for the wedding and the guest list had already been drawn.

Either Jeremy had the good sense to stay away for those two days, or it was as he professed, that he would be sequestered at his home in order to study his speech to be delivered before Parliament.

When the day finally arrived for his appearance before the combined Houses, Constance had a case of the jitters. She would have longed to be there to watch him, but she knew it would serve only to frazzle his nerves. Arguments or no, she already missed him, but she knew that if he couldn't call on her earlier, she was sure to see him that night at Almack's.

The hands on the clock moved slowly.

Millicent was no help. She sat in a comfortable chair in Constance's sitting room, one eye on her tatting, the other on Constance. Finally she put her needlework down. "There. You've made me drop another stitch. You've done nothing but pace the floor for the last ten minutes. Jeremy, assuming he can escape from his admirers, couldn't possibly arrive for at least another two hours.''

''I know. But I'm so unsettled I can't sit still.'' She sank to the floor at her aunt's knees. ''I've decided to accept his bid for me—if indeed he asks me properly.''

Millicent snorted. ''What more can he say? He's made it pretty clear that he wants to marry you.'' She stroked Constance's hair. ''Be smart, girl. Don't frighten him off with your stubbornness.''

''He's not easily fright—'' She was interrupted by the sound of flying gravel and a carriage entering the driveway at high speed. A horse whinnied as the carriage stopped abruptly. Constance got up and ran to her window and threw back the draperies.

''Dear heaven. It's Jeremy. He looks . . . Something must have gone wrong.''

Apparently seeing the movement at her window, Jeremy stopped dead and stared up at her, unsmiling. Then, taking the steps two at a time, he flung open the double doors and charged up the stairs to her quarters.

Constance opened her door just in time to see him striding down the hallway. It was clear that he was in a towering rage.

Her heart went out to him as she allowed him entry to her sitting room. ''What is it, Jeremy? What happened? Were they displeased with your speech?''

''You! You Jezebel! Do you have any idea what you have done to me?'' He approached her as if he were about to strike her.

Millicent stood. "My lord! Do control yourself."

Constance reached behind her for the edge of the dresser. Her knees had suddenly gone weak. "I don't understand. What are you talking about, Jeremy?"

"Egad. You said you'd get even, but I didn't think you'd be quite so vindictive." He flung the morning newspaper on the floor.

Constance reached down to pick it up. There, on the front page, was a copy of the caricature she had drawn of Jeremy, her name scrawled across the bottom in bold script.

He took her by the shoulders. "Are you satisfied? Wait till you hear the rest. When I stood to address Parliament, someone brayed like a donkey, and suddenly the room, the entire room, erupted in uncontrollable laughter."

"Oh, Jeremy," Constance wailed.

He dropped his hands from her shoulder and walked to the window to rest his hand against the frame. "There was no quieting them. Every time I started to speak the laughter began again. Finally I gave up and had to sit down. No. I had to, in fact, leave the premises in order for them to carry on the business of the Crown." He swore. "And I have you to thank for it."

Constance put out her hands to him. "No, Jeremy. I had nothing to do with it."

"I suppose the caricature came to life and walked all the way to Fleet Street on its own!"

And with that, he shrugged her hand away and strode from the room, down the stairs and out of the house. Constance followed him as far as the stairway.

Downstairs, Stavers stared open-mouthed first at Jeremy, then at her.

Try as they would the women could find no explanation for how the cartoon came to be published in the London *Times*. True, cartoons were the lifeblood of the newspaper, but Cruikshank, with his wiry lines and dark shading, was becoming nearly as popular as Gillray had been in his day. Why would the newspaper stoop to use the work of an amateur? And how did it acquire the cartoon in the first place?

Constance laced her fingers together in front of her to keep them from shaking. "The last I remember seeing the sketchbook, it was being passed around the room at Marlborough House for everyone to look at."

"Then one of the guests must have pinched it," Millicent said. "I'm sure that no one from the duke's establishment would be so cruel." She smacked her hand on the table. "But we know who would, now, don't we?"

Constance was surprised. "Who?"

"Why, Lady Francine, of course. Did you see the look on her face when Jeremy swore he was going to marry you? She was as pale as mould at the bottom of a well."

Constance shook her head. "No. I don't think she could have done it. She would never want to hurt Jeremy like that. Not if she loves him."

Millicent sniffed and gave her a significant look. For the moment, there seemed to be no other answer.

THE PARTY THAT NIGHT at Almack's was supposed to be in Jeremy's honour. The question uppermost in

Constance's head all afternoon was whether or not he would be there, let alone stop by for her in his carriage. She was sure everyone would credit her with the cartoon fiasco, in just the way Jeremy had. She wouldn't try to defend herself, but nor could she allow the haut ton to talk behind her back.

As chance would have it, his carriage arrived well ahead of the appointed time. Stavers climbed the stairs to the bedroom and handed his message to Lacey, who passed it on to Constance.

"'E's ere, I'll wager," Lacey said, "an' your 'air still down round yer waist." She clucked her tongue. "Well, go on an' open it."

Constance unfolded the note, then slowly folded it again. Her throat was dry and her voice cracked when she spoke. "It seems Lord Jeremy is not coming to take us to Almack's after all. He will be there, however, and he sends his regrets about not escorting us."

"I say! What a bounder 'e turned out to be. A pox on 'im and 'is likes."

"No. It's not his fault."

"Huh!"

The news was passed on to Millicent, and in the end they decided it would cause less gossip to go without him than not to put in an appearance at all.

Millicent was crushed. "I can't understand his behaviour."

"He has a great deal of pride, and he was so honoured to have an opportunity to address Parliament. To be brought down like that..." Constance sat on the edge of the bed. "I can't blame him for striking out at everyone close at hand." She blinked quickly to hide her tears. "I would give anything not to have to go to the party."

Millicent put her hands on her hips. "Well, we're going, my girl, and that's that. Take off your dress."

"What?"

"Do as I say." She whipped out of the room to return a few minutes later with the most elegant gown Constance had ever seen. It was a shimmering peach colour in a heavenly Chinese silk with a delicate lace shawl.

Millicent undid the catches. "I had it made for you from the bolt of silk you liked so much. This seems a good time to bring it out."

Constance rose and held the dress against her. "It's...it's exquisite. Perfect!" Constance hugged her aunt. "How can I ever thank you?"

"Just put it on, girl. We don't have all evening. While you get ready I'll have the carriage brought around."

Between the three of them, Constance was dressed, powdered and perfumed in record time. They arrived at Almack's only fashionably late. The crowd was already there in anticipation of an unforgettable evening. Constance, tall as she was, could see over the heads of many of the elegantly attired guests, but there was no sign of Jeremy. She lacked the nerve to enquire, but finally Lady Smithfield took her aside.

"He's here, my dear. In the anteroom."

"How is he?"

"Distraught."

"I suppose Lady Francine is comforting him?"

Lady Smithfield fluttered her fan. "She is not one to miss an opportunity. Or to miss creating one."

Constance paled. "Indeed? Was it she, do you think, who gave the cartoon to the press?"

Her Ladyship shrugged. "My dear, I only know it wasn't you."

Constance was grateful for her trust. "The point is Jeremy doesn't believe that."

"Doesn't he? Well, you will soon find out, my dear. He's coming this way. If you'll excuse me I'll leave the two of you alone."

Jeremy met her gaze from across the room and held it until he was at her side. He took her hands in his hands and massaged the palms with his thumbs.

"It seems I have a lot to learn about falling in love."

Constance looked up at him, her eyes dark with pain. He cleared his throat but it was still husky. "I don't know how to say this, but once again, I spoke too quickly. I misjudged you and I beg your forgiveness."

"Then you know who was responsible for putting the cartoon in the paper?"

"No. Not yet. I only know you would never do such a thing. I love you. I trust you. It's as simple as that."

"Oh, Jeremy." She was too moved to say more.

His mouth twisted in a forced smile. "'Oh, Jeremy'? Is that all you have to say?"

"I . . . I don't know. What do you want from me?"

He looked surprised. "I want you to say you love me and that you will consent to be my wife."

"I . . . I do love you."

A sudden light warmed his indigo eyes. "And you will marry me?"

She half turned away. "I want to but...but I am so afraid that once we're married I will lose you to some other woman. I couldn't stand to be married to a womanizer, the way my mother was."

He took her chin in his hand and turned her head to face him. "A moment ago I spoke of my trust in you. Trust is a two-headed swan, my love. It looks both ways. How could I want anyone else when I've waited all my life for you?"

She shook her head, blinking rapidly.

"Then say it, my love. Say you will be my wife."

She took a deep breath. "If you truly want me, I will marry you."

He let out a whoop that turned several faces in their direction. "It's done, then. No backing out?"

She smiled. "Not on my part."

"I'd like to tell my godmother before the betrothal becomes common knowledge. And of course I will want to consult with your aunt."

Constance pressed her hands together in front of her. "You may be a trifle late. From the expressions I see around us, I have the feeling that quite a number of people already know."

He grinned, then made a low sweeping bow to those who were watching them. There was a round of applause from the gentlemen and more than few envious glances from the women. Constance smiled, willing her heart to stop racing.

Although no one chose to breach etiquette by asking point-blank if the couple was betrothed, the atti-

tude in the room changed perceptibly for the better.
Talk centred on Jeremy's aborted attempt to address
Parliament, and he was assured by those in power that
he would be given another chance.

One irreverent soul stood at the top of the stairs and
called down to Constance that the editor of the paper
wanted to see her about buying her cartoons. There
was a shocked silence until someone else said that she
might need the work in order to support all the children she and Jeremy were sure to have.

The laughter eased the tension and a short time later
the music and dancing began.

Jeremy took her hand. "Would you be devastated
if I asked you to leave with me now? I'll send your
carriage home and the three of us can share mine. I
want to be alone with you."

She looked into his eyes. "Whatever you say."

He kissed her hand. "Wait here while I get our
wraps and inform your aunt."

Constance settled herself in a chair somewhat away
from the crowded dance floor. No sooner was she
seated than Lady Francine took a chair next to her.

"I hope you realize you are never going to marry
him."

"That remains to be seen, doesn't it? Was it you
who tore the cartoon from my sketchbook and presented it to the editor of the *Times*?"

"I admit nothing, but I will do anything, anything,
to prevent you from stealing Jeremy away from me."

"I doubt that you ever had him. If you did, he
wouldn't have waited this long to marry. Leave us
alone, Lady Francine. You can't hurt us anymore."

Lady Francine fumbled in her reticule and brought out an envelope. "Don't be too certain about that. Consider how this might look in the next issue of the *Times*."

Constance drew the page of foolscap from the envelope. It was a cartoon, drawn by Cruikshank, of Constance standing in front of The Tart Shoppe. She was holding her gown high enough to reveal a pair of knobby knees and a scandalous bit of unmentionables. But it was the sly, impish smile on her face that made her look like a member of the demimonde.

She tore it into shreds and placed them in the envelope.

Lady Francine looked smug. "It was only a copy. I have others, one for each of the newspapers if you continue to pursue Jeremy."

Constance hesitated long enough for Francine to see her indecision. "If you aren't concerned about your own reputation, think what the gossip will do to your aunt and to Jeremy. He has just recently come into his own. His reputation in court cannot survive another major scandal."

She stood before Constance could reply. "I'll give you twenty-four hours to prove to me that you've broken off with Jeremy. After that I take the drawings to the newspapers."

Jeremy approached with their cloaks just as Lady Francine brushed past him and blew a kiss in his direction.

Constance, too numb even to think beyond Lady Francine's threat, allowed him to put the cloak around her shoulders.

They were halfway home when Jeremy leaned forward. "All right, my dear, what is it?"

She shrugged. "Nothing I care to talk about."

"Is it our betrothal?"

She looked over at Millicent, who smiled benignly. Jeremy drew his hand across his moustache and looked sheepishly at Constance. "I'm sorry. I had to tell her. It was too good to keep to myself."

Constance felt the strain in her voice. "You're being a little premature, aren't you, sir? As a matter of fact I'm having second thoughts."

"The devil you are! Something's happened. What is it?"

"It's nothing."

He opened the flap to the driver and ordered him to pull over to the side of the road. "Now, Lady Constance," he said, reaching for her hands and holding them fast between his, "we spoke about trust. How about telling me the truth? I swear we will not budge an inch until you answer me."

She darted her tongue across her lips and tried to stall for time, but it was no use. He would not relent until she told him everything.

No sooner was the truth out than he ordered the driver to return to Almack's. So, he thought. Arabella *was* exacting her revenge, for doubtless it was she who contrived to release the juicy tidbit about Constance's night at The Tart Shoppe. His fury, however, was directed at Lady Francine.

His mouth hardened into a thin line. "There has to be some way to stop her. One thing is for sure. I'm going to let her know what I think of her."

They were only minutes away from Almack's, but the ride seemed much longer. When they arrived, Jeremy jumped down and warned the women to stay in the carriage until he returned.

"I'll do no such thing," Constance retorted. She swung herself down before he could attempt to stop her. Millicent followed but allowed the footman to assist her.

Jeremy swore softly, then apologized. "I would much prefer it if you would let me see to this alone."

"Never. You look far too agitated. I would fear for the woman's life."

"As well you might."

Once they were inside, they saw Lady Francine entering one of the anterooms with a group of her followers. They were laughing and appeared to be thoroughly enjoying themselves.

"Wait here," Jeremy said to Constance as he strode toward them.

She ignored his order and followed close behind, with Millicent bringing up the rear.

Jeremy entered the room, which was occupied by perhaps fifteen or twenty people. Their conversation dwindled when they saw his face. He stood tall and straight, locking his hands behind him, in a commanding pose.

"I would be grateful if you would excuse us. I would like to have a private word with Lady Francine."

The room was dead silent and no one moved. Lady Francine's father stepped forward. "Now see here, St.

James. You have no right to speak to us that way. Are you foxed or have you gone daft?''

Jeremy's voice dropped to a deadly pitch. "I've asked you once. I'll not ask again. Get out now, before I throw you out.''

Lady Francine laughed easily. "Don't you adore a strong man? Now run along, everyone. Jeremy and I have things to say to each other. You, too, father. I'll be quite safe. Jeremy's bark is worse than his bite.''

There was a sudden exodus from the room. Moments later, the four of them—Jeremy, Francine, Constance and Millicent—were left alone.

Jeremy wasted no time in telling Francine exactly what he thought of her dishonourable and childish tactics. She lifted her chin.

"Be that as it may, but you will change your mind. We belong together, Jeremy. We always have. Everyone knows that.''

"Only because you've convinced them. I never once gave you any indication that we were more than good friends. Now you've destroyed even that.''

"If that's the way you want it, than I shall also destroy the three of you.'' She was holding a wine glass in her hand. Before anyone could stop her, she threw it crashing against the wall, scant inches from where Constance was standing.

Jeremy grabbed Lady Francine's arm and held it roughly.

Constance came toward them, determination written on her face. "Let her go, Jeremy. She can't hurt us.''

Francine laughed and rubbed her arm. "Just watch the newspapers and see if I can't."

Constance nodded. "You have a point, but I warn you, Lady Francine, if we go down, you will fall with us. It seems I have a talent for caricature. The papers have offered to buy my cartoons, all of them. I wonder how you would look riding a broomstick. Or better still, as an old hag in her diamonds, chasing after Jeremy and our children. Or—"

Francine held up her hands. "Enough. I can't fight you. You have no breeding. No sense of class. And you, Jeremy. They were right when they said you would never amount to anything."

She jerked away from him and nearly ran to the door. Once there she opened it and said in a voice that carried across the entire ballroom, "I'm through with you, Jeremy St. James. I wouldn't marry you if you were the last person on earth." She slammed the door before they could answer.

Jeremy turned to look at Constance. She smiled and looked at Millicent. Of one accord they burst out laughing.

LESS THAN A MONTH LATER Jeremy and Constance were wed in a ceremony attended by nearly a hundred of the cream of London society. When it was over he lifted her into the carriage and climbed in next to her. His knee bumped hers and he started to pull away, then remembered.

"Egad. I don't know how to behave without your chaperon standing guard over you."

Constance regarded him dryly. "I doubt that you have forgotten, but in case you have, I suspect we could consult with Madame Duprey."

His eyes sparkled. "Now there's an idea."

He reached into his pocket. "We owe a lot to her, you know. But we owe a real debt of gratitude to the tainted pigeon pie that brought us together.

"And just so we will never forget..." He placed a lovely jewel box in her hands. When she lifted the lid she gasped in amazement. There, resting on a pillow of blue velvet, was a brooch shaped like a pigeon in flight. It was made of diamonds and rubies and silver filigree; a perfect size to wear on a gown or on the crown of a wide-brimmed hat.

"I've never seen anything so exquisitely delicate," she said.

"I had it made especially for you."

She put the cover back on the box and studied his face. "I wonder, will you miss your old life? Will you be sorry you settled for a wife instead of a...a tart?"

He leaned over and kissed her, softly at first, then with ever-increasing warmth. At last he sat back. "What a question, my love! In you I have everything—beauty, intelligence, compassion...and to think I had the added bonus of finding you in The Tart Shoppe." His eyes twinkled, then he added, "What more could a man ask?"

Constance laughed, then gave a sigh of happiness. What more indeed?

Harlequin Regency Romance™

COMING NEXT MONTH

#5 COUSIN NANCY by Alberta Sinclair
Nancy Browne is a penniless orphan, but everyone
loves her for her natural country charm and
spontaneous good humour. When she arrives at the
country estate of her cousins, she is introduced to their
neighbour, the Earl of Selbridge. She is promptly
smitten but fears a match impossible, being poor and
without position. Little does she know this matters not
to the Earl, who returns her affection secretly. To win
the Earl she must prove herself to be a proper lady. She
does not reckon on his perplexing reaction.

#6 FALSE IMPRESSIONS by Margaret Westhaven
Being twenty and nine, Theodora Thornfield decides to
accept a position as paid companion to her cousin and
go to London. She does not expect to attract any
suitors, but Mr. Lawrence Carruthers, a handsome,
wealthy landowner, wastes no time in bespeaking his
interest in her. Dora is flattered until she learns that
Mr. Carruthers means to make her his next mistress.
Dora owns that she may be "on the shelf," but never
would she be that desperate!

ANNOUNCING . . .

The Lost Moon Flower
by Bethany Campbell

Look for it this August
wherever Harlequins are sold

HR 3000-1